MW00912589

# WHAT HAPPENED NEXT CHANGED MANY LIVES

*To Donna*

LENORA KLAPPE

*Lenora Klappe*

for info: lenoraklappe.com

 FriesenPress

One Printers Way
Altona, MB R0G 0B0
Canada

www.friesenpress.com

ISBN
978-1-03-913612-0 (Hardcover)
978-1-03-913611-3 (Paperback)
978-1-03-913613-7 (eBook)

1. *Fiction, Crime*

Distributed to the trade by The Ingram Book Company

PROLOGUE

# SPRING 1990

Coach Bruce Palmer was tense. The basketball team from Deer Lake High School had had a very good year. It seemed the provincial title was possible again this year. He was proud of how the team had gelled. Teamwork, team spirit, and team pride had been deeply instilled in the players. They easily won the quarter final and semi-finals, and now they were on to the finals, facing a team that had started out the year as underdogs but had found their "mojo" and rallied through to the finals.

Coach Palmer had a lot riding on the outcome of the final game: his job as coach, the future of his players, and the pride of the town. Bruce knew he was losing his star players as they would be graduating. He also knew that sport scouts would be in the crowd. They had a strong team and hometown advantage, and they were the defending team. The gym was packed to capacity. The whole town was pumped. Businesses, homes, and vehicles were adorned in the team colours of orange and blue. The air was electric.

Bruce was much tenser this year than last year. The final game had been held in the rural community of Rangeland, a two-hour drive away. His team had been the favourite to win, and they did by over thirty points.

He realized the players were ready and waiting for his instructions. Brad Andrew, his star, was in great spirits, cool and confident. Phil Albright, his second-best player, seemed tense and anxious.

"Okay team, listen up. This is the game we have spent all term working up to. We have a flawless record, strong teammates, and a whole town pulling for us. As defending champs for the third time, we have a lot of pressure to deal with. Remember, you are a team, not individual players. We have practised a lot of manoeuvers that play like a dance. Do not think of anything but the game and the strategic plays that we have spent time on and that have led to our many wins. Above all, remember who else might be in the bleachers tonight. Go get 'em!"

The team lined up ready to enter the gym where the cheerleaders were performing. Led by Monika

Johnson and wearing cute blue and orange outfits, they were waving pompoms and chanting:

*Deer Lake Deer Lake*
*Make no mistake*
*Deer Lake Deer Lake*
*It's yours to take!!*

On the other side of the gym, the Rangeland cheerleaders dressed in red and white were also dancing and chanting:

*Rangeland Rangeland*
*You know you can*
*Rangeland Rangeland*
*We know you can!!*

When the cheerleaders were finished, players from both sides ran into the centre of the gym, shook hands and stood for the singing of the school songs and the Canadian anthem.

The whistle blew to start the game. It was a nail-biter game as the lead changed many times. The teams were evenly matched.

The first quarter saw both teams playing a tight game, passing and dribbling like a well-rehearsed dance. After eight minutes, the game was scoreless. Coach Palmer was pleased with how the players were conducting themselves as a team but disappointed at the score. He advised them on what manoeuvers to use next.

After the second period, both teams came alive, finishing with Deer Lake scoring inside and outside the line for a total of fifteen points. They also had one point for a throw from the foul line as one player from Rangeland had double dribbled.

By the end of the third period, the score had jumped to forty to thirty-six in favour of Deer Lake. The players were feeling the pressure. Coach made a few changes to the team line up but now decided only his strongest players would be on the court for the final minutes. Phil had committed two violations in the first period. Brad and Mark were playing excellent games. These three needed to continue to work together as the clock was running out.

It was the last play of the last game of the tournament. Tension consumed the crowd as the game was tied with less than a minute to go. Phil Albright was frantic. This was to be his final chance to impress the university athletic scouts who were sure to be in the crowd.

For four long years of high school, Brad Andrew, his best friend and rival, had been MVP and team captain. He was a 'shoo in' for the sports scholarship. Time was quickly running out for Phil to be the one to save the game and win the undying gratitude of the school. It was now or never. Phil looked up from his position close to the net. Martin Brown had the ball. He dribbled and threw the ball towards Phil. But in a nanosecond, Brad raced over, intercepted the ball, and threw it to the net. The ball caught and tottered on the rim. The noisy crowd was suddenly quiet as all eyes watched the ball hesitate then fall through the net. The resulting roar drowned out the final whistle. Once again, Brad ruled the court and commanded the love of the school and the town. He owned the victory.

His teammates lifted him onto their shoulders and paraded around the gym. Brad was overjoyed—a king was crowned.

Monika Johnson was thrilled that Brad had once again saved the team. She started towards him, cutting into the crush of exuberant fans, but she was pushed aside. She was shocked and embarrassed when her shouts to him went unanswered. Monika could not believe her eyes. For over twelve years, she and Brad had shared all their victories together. Tonight was his biggest win yet and he did not wait for her. Stunned, she ran outside and curled up in confusion.

Meanwhile back at the gym, Principal Setters was trying desperately to get everyone's attention. Finally he used the bull horn to quiet the crowd. Coach Palmer was attempting to assemble his team. Brad was still being mobbed and searching the gym for Monika, Martin was laughing and hugging his family, Phil was just entering the gym.

Mr. Setters thanked everyone for attending the game. He called the principal and coach of the Rangeland team to come to the podium.

"I would like to thank Deer Lake High School and the whole town for being great hosts to our team. We will be back next year with different results." promised the principal. The crowd applauded. "Coach did an excellent job bringing our team from the bottom to the finals."

The Rangeland team left the stage after accepting silver medals. The Deer Lake team entered.

Mr. Setters once again restored order. "I must say that was a game for the history books. What a legacy for the school team. I now call Coach Palmer."

When the shouting calmed down, Coach Palmer lined up the team, noting that Brad was still searching for Monika. He thanked his team, handed out the gold medals. The provincial trophy was presented to Brad as team captain. Brad handed the trophy to Martin to hold while he received the MVP award.

Mr. Setters gave up trying to restore order for the final comments. He turned off the PA system and went into the crowd.

Once the crowd frenzy dissipated, Brad spotted Monika emerging from the changing room. He ran to her in a panic, frantic that he did not know where she had been—wondering why she was not there to share his victory and see him receive the MVP trophy as well as the Championship trophy.

Monika explained that she thought he had ignored her. "I thought you were so caught up in the victory that you did not need me by your side"

Brad was stunned by her statement. "I was falling off the shoulders of the guys. Once I was stable, I looked for you, but you were nowhere to be seen. I waved at our parents. I will always need and want you with me. We have known we belong together for over twelve years." He gave her a hug and said, "I am going to clean up. Wait for me in the hallway."

While Brad went to shower and change, he wondered why Monika appeared deep in thought. Her eyes seemed red and swollen as if she had been the crying.

When Brad returned, they got into his car. He was shocked when she suggested that instead of going home they drive to his parents' business site where they could have some privacy.

He would always remember her words well. "Brad, for the last month or so, there seems to be an underlying tension between us."

He readily agreed. "Absolutely. I thought it was because we are both concerned with graduating from high school and making a big life change to continue our education. I've been afraid that we may end up in different universities. I am glad you have also felt the pressure."

Monika then blew him away with what she said next.

"After what happened tonight, I think we need to discuss our long time promise of celibacy. We are adults now and totally committed to each other, have been forever. The possibility of going to separate universities is causing us a lot of anxiety. We're also old enough to have sexual awareness and to understand our needs. I think we should seriously consider abandoning our vow of celibacy and relieve ourselves of the physical and emotional tension between us."

It did not take Brad long to be persuaded. At first, they clung to each other in the front seat of the car, convincing each other that it was the right decision.

Before long, they were in the backseat of the car kissing and groping and not quite knowing what to do. Their mouths pressed together frantically. Monika straddled Brad's lap as both realized they were really going to make love. They tore at each other's clothes. Thank goodness the elastic waistbands made getting naked a lot easier. Before long, they were two sweaty bodies with tangled limbs and heavy breathing coming together in awkwardness. It was not romantic, but it was releasing. When it was over, they were spread out on the seat. Neither of them could believe what had just happened. The physical and emotional toll left them hugging each other in shock. Slowly, they started to kiss. Soon they began touching and exploring every part of each other. They enjoyed the smell, sight and feel of sex. The tension grew as they continued all the actions that were so new to them. They exploded together in a fury of passion that left then laughing and crying in sheer wonder.

They then discovered how messy sex was. In their duffle bags they found towels and other clothes to disguise the evidence of sex. They knew once home, their parents would be waiting for them.

Life was oh so much better now. The tension was gone. Slowly, they cleaned up, redressed, and headed for home. They could not believe what they had been denying themselves. The intimacy continued as soon as Brad was courageous enough to buy condoms. He remembered being shocked at the myriad choices: colour, shape, lubricated, themed. Who knew?

What happened next changed many lives.

# CHAPTER ONE

# SPRING 1990

Monika was feeling nostalgic as she sat in her bedroom—her private sanctuary. She looked around the room and smiled. It was so out of date. Was it only four years ago that she had decorated it her own way? How proud she had been of the overall look. Now that she would soon be leaving for university, she realized how juvenile the room looked.

The walls were a delicate shade of mauve; the curtains, which she helped her mom sew, had a floral print that picked up the wall colour. Her comforter was made of a complementary pattern. The closet was neatly arranged with her clothes hung by type: T-shirts, blouses, sweaters, skirts, and dresses. Boots, shoes, and slippers were lined up on the floor of the closet. Her chest of drawers was also well organized with her swimming clothes in one drawer, her soccer gear in another. Her undergarments, neatly stacked, filled the top drawer. Under the bed were storage bins housing her winter clothes.

One of her favourite items in the room was a cedar chest, a gift from her Granma. It was a classic piece of furniture full of memories of a wonderful lady. Her maternal grandparents, the McAdams, had lived next door and spoiled her and her sister Mavis a lot. Granpa and Granma were a big part of her child-hood. Monika's parents, Flo and Doug Johnson, were both CPAs and owned their own business. Especially during tax season, the girls spent a lot of time next door. Granma was a textbook grandmother teach-ing them to make cookies, driving them to lessons, helping with teenage angst, and just loving them. Granpa was also super. He took the girls fishing, taught them throwing and catching, and even took them golfing. Ten years ago, when Granpa retired, the McAdams sold all of their possessions and joined a Christian funded mission, volunteering in Africa. That was when Monika inherited the beautiful chest. She cared for it lovingly, polishing it annually. In it, along with other precious items, she kept all the cor-respondence that she received from Africa.

Monika shook her head and returned to the tour of her room. She focused on the shelf holding yearbooks that showcased her many achievements, as well as Brad's. The wall above the shelf showcased a dozen ribbons testifying to her triumphs in soccer and swimming. Beside those were awards from her school for good citizenship and top academics, including one for the Gauss Math Competition in grade eight and one for the Canadian National Spelling Bee in grade three. There were leadership awards from the church for her work with the Sunday school and with the teen program. Her biggest trophy was for being the team captain of the winning soccer team at the provincial tournament last year.

The one heartache of her youth was her tenth birthday. Despite her tearful pleadings and promises to be extra good and helpful, her parents did not relent and let her have a dog. They explained how there was no time to walk a dog or play with it. The household schedule was already strained as both parents worked and the girls had to be transported to school, lessons, and practices.

Continuing her surveillance of her room, Monika focused on all the photos lining one wall. Most of them had Brad Andrew in them. Monika and Brad had met in preschool and formed a bond that was still so strong they knew their futures would always be together.

She recalled the many outings her family had shared with Brad's over the years. Both families owned cabins up at the lake and spent many happy times there. Together, they learned to swim, water ski, pilot a boat, and fish. Her albums were filled with pictures of her Mom and Dad, Mavis, and of course, Brad and his family: Joe and Mary Andrew and Brad's sister Kristie. Both families lived in the same area, attended the same church, and participated in many community events. Monika and Brad had their futures already planned: high school, university, then marriage and a family.

A big smile covered Monika's face as she looked at her favourite photo of Brad and her both holding fish they had caught. She remembered that day very well. It had been a family fishing derby. Brad had bragged that he had the biggest fish until it was compared it to Monika's. Brad tried very hard to hide his feelings and managed a smile for the camera. Then his demeanor changed, and he walked off to be alone for a while. His mom gave him a minute to deal with his disappointment then called him back to the campfire.

Thinking of the future brought her mind back to the present. Her desk was cluttered with university and scholarship application forms waiting to be filled in and sent off.

A sharp knock on the door was followed by Mavis storming in with an announcement her long blonde ponytail swinging back and forth as she methodically toured the room.

"As soon as you leave, I'm taking over this room. It is so much nicer and bigger than mine. You better pack up all your bling. I'm turning the room into a shrine to all my favourite movie stars and musicians. First the wall colour gets changed to something less girlie. No more drapes but neat blinds. Then this room will be modernized and personalized to ME." Mavis then danced around the room touching everything and saying, "Gone" to all of Monika's prized possessions.

"Fine," answered Monika, "But you better not ruin Granma McAdam's cedar chest. It goes with me when Brad and I get married in five years. Now, take your enthusiasm and get out as I have a lot of work to do. I need to be prepared to leave in the fall. Scat." Mavis continued her study of the room. From the window she muttered, "Nicer view than my room," and from the corner said, "Nicer closet that mine. Soon it will be all MINE and your presence will disappear."

Monika began to wonder what she would miss about the town she had lived in all her life. Deer Lake was a small town that was eighty kilometres from the lake of the same name. The town was situated at the crossroads of two major traffic routes lined with motels and fast food outlets. From May to September, the population of the town nearly doubled with visitors arriving to take advantage of the warmer climate and to enjoy all sorts of water sports. Many tourists owned cabins on the lake that they returned to year after year. The Johnsons had been given one of these cabins nearly twenty years ago when Doug's parents moved to Victoria. They spent most long weekends and holidays there. The only big vacations they went on were to visit Flo's parents in whatever exotic African country they were currently managing a mission in.

Now Monika really had to quit reminiscing and planning as it was time to leave for her weekend job as a lifeguard at the Deer Lake Community Centre. Swimming had always been a big part of her life both at the lake and at the pool. For six years, she had been active in the swim club, always enhancing her skills. She had qualified as a lifeguard two years ago and had been working as a guard on weekends and holidays ever since. She was also working on her certificate as a swim coach. Between homework, practices, and work, there was little time left for idle thoughts.

With one last wistful look at her room, she picked up her duffel bag and checked to make sure it contained her bathing suit, bathing cap, towel, and the toiletries she would require. She checked her appearance in the full-length mirror to ensure her hair was well pinned and her official employee T-shirt matched her shorts. With one more quick look at Brad's picture, she frowned a bit. Lately, she was noticing that he seemed intense and even moody at times.

She decided it was because school days were nearly over and big changes were about to affect their lives.

She grabbed the keys to her scooter and left her room, calling a quick "goodbye" to her mother and sister as she left the house. Monika had purchased a scooter two years ago to relieve the complex transportation needs of the busy family. She could get herself to all the places she needed to be without disturbing her mom or dad, who could not always leave the office. On occasion, she would also pick up or deliver Mavis. Her scooter was her prize possession. It came from Apex Auto Wreckers and Scrap Yard, the Andrew family business, as a discard, but had many more kilometres left in it. Her parents had paid for half the repairs. Once it passed safety inspection, it was hers, and she rode it as much as possible to cut down on carpools, buses, and walking. It was a bright yellow, so she called it "Sunshine."

\*\*\*

Brad Andrew was daydreaming again. Planning his future life was one of his favourite pastimes, especially because it included Monika. He knew she was his soul mate the day he first saw her at pre-school.

He was currently trying to decide what scholarships and universities to apply for but predicted that no matter where he went, his life would continue to be full of successes. In five years, he would either be a pro athlete or an accredited basketball coach. No matter what he did - be it academics, sports, or student politics- he excelled with ease. His room was overwhelmed with ribbons, trophies, plaques, and other kudos attesting to these successes. Next to these were pictures of him with Monika from kindergarten to the present. He had never cared about redecorating his room, so remnants of youthful sports-themed wallpaper were still visible behind all the certificates and posters. A net hanging in the corner contained all of his prized stuffies from over the years. There was even a box of Lego building blocks still in the corner. His mother had long ago quit trying to make him tidy his room to her standards. As long as he kept the door closed and the window open, she left him alone.

Brad returned to filling in the forms as he was due at the yard to help his dad. Summer was a busy time for the family company. The business was located in the industrial part of town, and because of the town's location adjacent to two busy highways, there were many calls for the services of the business, especially in snow season. Joe and Mary Andrew had started their business with one tow truck twenty years ago. Over the years, they bought land for a compound, then heavy duty equipment to begin the wrecking and parts divisions. Brad had been working at the yard for most of his life. He was now in charge of cleaning out all personal belongings in a vehicle before it moved on to the next step. Brad was allowed to keep any small change found in the vehicles. Other items were identified and sealed and then kept in a box for three months; some questionable items that could be considered suspect or illegal were locked in a secure box for transfer to the RCMP.

The phone rang, snapping him out of his daydreaming.

"Hi, Mom. What's up?"

"Brad, before you come into work today could you please pick up your sister at the community centre and drive her to the Johnsons'? Kristie and Mavis have plans for the day. Do not hang around so you can visit Monika!"

"Okay, I'm about to leave here now."

Brad had one slightly annoying little sister Kristie, who was just as successful in all her endeavors as he was in his. While Brad excelled in team sports, Kristie was a star at dance, gymnastics, and equestrian skills. Whereas Brad's after school activities were primarily at the school, Kristie always had to be driven to another location. On rare occasions, Brad had to drive her to her venue before he could gear up for his practice. But then, she was cute and sweet and easy to love so he subdued his annoyed feelings, drove her to where she needed to be, gave her a hug, and rushed back to his practice.

He quickly changed from his school T-shirt and shorts to the clothes necessary for working a dirty demolition station. He took one last look around his room then made a quick stop at the bathroom before heading out the door. The bathroom was the other annoying issue in his life. His parents had an ensuite bathroom, but he and his sister Kristie had to share the main bathroom. It wasn't a problem until she became a teenager and started to accumulate so many cosmetics that she was slowly taking over the entire room. *Well*, he thought, *a couple more months and I'll be gone to university. She can have as much room as she needs.* With one last look around to make sure the house was secure, Brad grabbed his keys and headed to the driveway where his car was parked.

Brad slowly backed his car out of the driveway. It was his first car, and he was sure that for the rest of his life, it would be his favourite. He headed for the community centre to pick up Kristie and Mavis. The two girls had been best friends for years, and were almost always together. Fortunately, they were both waiting for him with their duffel bags containing swimsuits, towels, and other essentials. Both girls were wearing their school T-shirts and cut-off shorts. Even their shoes were the same. They could pass for twins. The girls jumped into the car, Kristie in the front and Mavis in the back. Nothing had interrupted their conversation. They carried on chatting for the entire trip

10

to the Johnson house. True to his promise, Brad did not stop the car and run in to see if Monika was home. He backed up and drove to the family business.

Brad parked his car by the office and made a quick stop inside to say hi to his mom and to assure her he had delivered the girls to the Johnson's home.

As usual, his dad was waiting with a long list of chores for him to do. Wearing his steel-toed boots, heavy overalls, and shirt and cap with the company logo, he smiled at his son. Years of hard physical labour had resulted in firm muscles and a permanently tanned face. Covering his head with baseball caps over time had rendered him bald.

"Brad, a new car came in. Clean it up, check for personal belongings, and drive or tow it over to the wrecking site."

"Okay, Dad. It sure looks like it had been a beauty when it was new."

Brad put on his working gloves and overalls before heading to the latest crashed car, a 1989 Ford.

\*\*\*

Phil Albright was exhausted. Preparing for final exams took a lot of time and energy. Keeping fit enough to maintain a spot on sports teams kept him at the gym. For the millionth time, he wished things would come as easily for him as they did for his friend Brad.

For the four years of high school, he had always come in second to Brad in sports and in academics. Brad had the perfect family whereas Phil's widowed father was an alcoholic, who, even though he was a skilled carpenter, could not keep a job. Their life was not ideal. His dad spent time at bars and strip joints and had little time or money for his son.

Phil's mother died from complications of a miscarriage when Phil was five years old. His father, John, was unable to cope. He fell into a drunken stupor and lost his job. John's parents took Phil into their home. Eighteen months later, John came to retrieve Phil as his parents felt it was time, plus they wanted to go on a cruise. During the time Phil lived with his grandparents, John had been forced to sell the family home and was living in a rented trailer. It was to be the first of many temporary homes.

When John went to register Phil for school, he learned that his parents had never sent Phil to school. The principal insisted that since he had received no formal education, it was best if Phil started in kindergarten rather than with children his own age. Thus Phil was forever more than a year older than his classmates.

Because he changed schools often, Phil knew how to size up the culture of a student body. When he had transferred into his latest school, he quickly surmised that Brad Andrew was king, so he set out to be his friend. It would be very hard work as they were from different social circles. However, they did become quite good friends through sports. Phil did not know if the friendship was based on charity, competition, or compatibility. Phil learned to live with the fact that Brad often teasingly called him Phil not-so-bright. It did not really matter. It was an ace he used to his benefit. Over the years, Phil had observed a side of Brad that not many others witnessed. Often after a practice or game that did not go well, Phil had seen Brad's confident, relaxed façade slip, showing annoyance bordering on anger.

An example of their differences was obvious: for his sixteenth birthday, Brad got a second-hand car that he and his dad had refurbished from the junk yard. It had been a fun bonding activity between father and son.

Not so at the Albright house. For his sixteenth birthday, Phil was given a second-hand ten-speed bike and told to get a job to help support the household. When Phil turned eighteen, his dad bought him a case of beer and a visit from a stripper. She came to the house with all the tools of the trade, and boy did she teach him a lot. There were videos, lotions, provocative clothing, and condoms. When she left, he was in a state of amazed exhaustion. He was addicted to sex from then on. His girlfriend Mandy Fleming did not put out, but in the months that followed, he learned that a lot of the sports groupies did.

Not only did Phil have to study and exercise a lot, but he also had to work long hours at the local grocery store. There was no university fund for him. He vowed to educate himself out of poverty. Scholarship was the only way he could go to a university instead of a college. He was hoping for a sport's scholarship in either basketball or track and field, as long as Brad did not win them all.

Oh well, back to the grind. Study one hour, run one hour, work two hours, study some more. Just as he got back to the books to study, his dad came in with a woman.

"Get out, sonny boy, Daddy has company, unless you want to stay and share. She is bought and paid for."

As much as he thought it was a good idea, Phil knew he had to study. Since he did not have a study area in his tiny bedroom, he often had to do home-work at the kitchen table or the town library. Before picking up the supplies he would need, he made a trip to his room. He carefully chose clothes to wear. He had used some of his precious savings to buy the latest fads. Leaving the house, he jumped onto his old relic of a bike. It got him places in the cheapest, fastest way.

He wondered if Mandy Fleming would also be at the library, as she also had nowhere to study at home. Her parents both worked at low paying jobs and did their best to provide for the family of four. There was no university fund there either. Both parents worked long hours, often with late shifts, leaving Mandy to do a lot of chores around the home. She wanted to be a nurse but had to study hard to get grades to qualify for financial help. There were no grandparents or Union affiliation to help. Student loans would have to be incurred, if she could qualify. Mandy had a sweet, kind countenance. She wasn't big on sports, but was a cheerleader and a library assistant. Phil and Mandy were friends with Brad and Monika despite the differences in their backgrounds. Whereas Phil played second fiddle to Brad, so did Mandy to Monika.

While at the library, Phil would fill out the applications for scholarships, bursaries, and universities, and then head to work at the grocery store. He did not think his chances of financial aid were great, but bursaries were sometimes based on need as well as ability.

Mandy was at the library, hard at work filling out her forms. She looked up and smiled at Phil as he entered the study area. She was definitely a girlfriend of convenience, not someone he felt he wanted as a partner. However, she served a purpose, as his friendship with her kept him in Monika and Brad's clique. He needed the social contact with the 'in' crowd as his way of learning the ways and mannerisms of people who were doing well.

"Hi Mandy," he whispered, knowing the librarian would be annoyed if he spoke in a normal voice. Mandy was seated at the corner carrel with her papers all neatly sorted for ease in filling in the forms. Her unruly curly hair was held out of her face by a colourful scrunchie. She removed her glasses to reveal her fresh, makeup-free face. Mandy was petite like the rest of her family. She was wearing faded denim capris, a striped T-shirt and plain runners, making her look a lot younger than her eighteen years.

"Hi, Phil. I was trying to work at home on the kitchen table but my sister and her friend were in the bedroom. I gave up and came here for some space and quiet."

"How are you making out with all the application forms?" asked Phil.

"Well, it would be better if I had a few more A's on my record. But other variables may work in my favour. There are some small bursaries I may qualify for like the Nurse's Union and the Hospital Auxiliary." For the past few years, Mandy had been a candy striper at the hospital and also worked part time at the hospital cafeteria. She seemed confident that having that information on her application form would help but had no idea about the number of others that may be in the competition for the awards.

Phil wandered over to an empty study carrel to begin studying the forms. His plan was to become a physical education teacher and coach. He was applying to the Teacher's Union and the Coach's Federation with the hopes of winning some funds to finance his dream.

***

Debbie Hartford was also thinking about graduation, but definitely not scholarships or bursaries. She just needed the bare minimum to earn enough credits to get a diploma. Science was her weakest subject. The teacher was not her favourite, but she knew a few flirty tricks would help her get a pass on the final. None of her courses were for entrance to university so there were no provincial exams.

The day had started out with yet another argument with her mother, Helen. The two of them had been arguing about homework since grade school.

Debra was one of the older members of her graduating class because she started school when she was six, not five like most of the other students. The first few years of her life had been difficult for her mom, a single mother with little in the way of marketable skills.

They had moved back in with Helen's mother in a very rural area where the nearest school was a long drive away. It would have made for a very tiring day for a five-year-old, so Helen kept Debra home. A year later, they moved to Deer Lake and Helen started working as a waitress.

"Deb, I'm going to work now, and I want you to do your homework. It is your last year and you need to graduate if you want any kind of decent job for the rest of your life." Her mother ordered. "You're over nineteen and should be contributing to the cost of running this house."

"Yeah, yeah, yeah, I know. Get a good job like wait-ressing for my life skill." She sassed back at her mom. "I remember what you told me last year. That I'm not smart enough for college or beautiful enough to marry well, so I need to find something I enjoy and learn to do it better than anyone else. I get it." Debbie sneered.

Ms. Hartford was wearing the uniform for the res-taurant that she had worked at for nearly fifteen years. She grabbed her purse and checked for her bus pass before issuing a final warning for Debra to get her homework done.

As soon as her mom left for work, Debbie went to her room and tried on her latest sexy outfit. She picked up her computer and set up at the kitchen table. Rather than do research for her school assign-ment, she began working on the web page she was constructing for herself. It showcased her in various poses wearing enticing garments.

Her concentration was interrupted when she heard the back door open. Damn.

Her mom must have forgotten something. She quickly covered up her outfit and closed her computer.

But it was not her mom, rather it was her mom's latest live-in boyfriend Ed. At least he was a decent looking guy, not like some who had passed through the house over the years.

"Hey kiddo, what's up? Are you actually doing homework? Let me see what subject you're researching. Maybe I can help"

"I doubt you know much about the life cycle of the moth. Why are you home so early? Did you lose your job like most of mom's special friends do?"

"No, smart aleck, I forgot my wallet. So let me see what you're studying." With that remark, he grabbed her computer and saw the page featuring her in various stages of undress.

"Now, now," he said. "What have we here? Maybe I can help you develop this page. How about we go to your room and check this out?"

The sexual activity between them had started a year ago when he first moved in. With her teenage hormones and his suave mannerisms, he soon had her learning all about flirting and foreplay. She was a willing student, and soon after that encounter, they arranged all sorts of meetings behind her mother's back. Her career choice was already made. No diploma necessary, free lessons courtesy of Ed and the internet.

That was how the first part of her education begun.

The second part came at high school. She glowed with her newfound experience and started hanging around the gym and attending school sports as a fan. The boys who had never looked at her before started noticing her now. Her new provocative manner and flirtatious ways had caught the eye of big shot basketball player Phil Albright. Her new outfits barely met the school dress code. Her long blonde hair flowed over her shoulders. Skillfully applied makeup defined her well-structured face.

"Hello there, sweetie. What is your name and where have you been hiding. Are you new here?" said Phil as he approached her.

"I'm not new to the school but I'm new to the sports scene. My name is Debra, but you can call me Debbie," she cooed. "I'm surprised I never knew how much fun watching jocks play could be. I noticed you and your smooth moves on the court," she added.

"I have many great moves, on and off the court. I can show you a few if you have time."

"I have all the time in the world," was her response.

They went into the now-empty changing room together. Between the lessons he received from his stripper teacher and the moves she learned from Ed, they had a very satisfactory experience that was to be one of many.

Before long, word spread, and Debbie was kept busy with many horny jocks. She continued to hone her talents by researching and watching porn. Her mom eventually kicked Ed out of the house when she suspected what was going on. Sometimes a boy would buy her a gift or take her for coffee, but her trysts were too much hobby and not enough career.

Part three of her education came just before graduation. She and Martin Brown were in his bedroom reenacting a scene from an X-rated movie when his dad, lawyer Walter Brown, unexpectedly came home. He heard noises in the bedroom so wondered why Martin was home. Needless to say, he was shocked when he entered the room and found the two kids engaged in a bizarre sex act.

"What in the world is going on in here?" he shouted. "Martin, go to my office now! Young lady put your clothes on and get into my car. I'm taking you home to your mother!"

Once in his car, Debra, instead of acting guilty, ashamed, or remorseful began to flirt with Walter. He looked over at her seductive pose and teasing eyes.

"Behave yourself, girl! Tell me where you live."

"Well, sir, first of all, I'm not a girl. I'm over nineteen. I live in Elm Manor, but no one is expecting me home yet," she simmered.

Martin felt himself responding to her behaviour, so instead of taking her home, he drove to one of his favourite out-of-town motels.

"Well, little one, how would you like to learn a few new adult moves instead of the fumbling moves of a teenager?" He proposed.

Coquettishly and with pretended inexperience, she allowed herself to be seduced by him. Later, Walter offered her taxi money to get home. The lesson she learned that day was that boys were fine but their dads had experience, wallets, and wives. Before long, her list of clients grew exponentially as Walter spread the word at the clubs he belonged to. The gifts she received were generous as they bought both merchandise and secrecy.

By high school graduation, Debbie already had a degree in her chosen field. There were no exams, no loans or textbooks, just a growing wardrobe and bank account. Plus a very interesting diary. Mom was right after all, find something you enjoy and be good at it.

CHAPTER TWO

# SUMMER 1990

Brad was in a great mood. He had been to the Vancouver Campus of UBC to register and have a tour of the facilities. Now he was on his way back to Deer Lake to share his news with Monika and his parents.

He had missed Monika so much, especially when she said that she was not feeling well.

That led his mind to wander and recall the great time he'd had at the graduation ceremonies. He remembered being stunned when he went to pick up Monika. He always knew she was beautiful, but that night, she was so absolutely gorgeous he could hardly breathe. Her hair was done in ringlets that settled around her face.

Wow, she actually had on a bit of makeup. She was wearing a fabulous blue, form-fitting dress that complemented her perfect figure and matched her eyes. He was sure glad he'd listened to his parents and worn a new suit with a tie that miraculously matched the colour of her dress.

The gym, decorated in the school colours was packed with the hundred grads, their families and the staff. The teens looked splendid in their formal dresses and suits.

The ceremony was perfect as they all received their diplomas, but the highlight was when Brad got a special mention for his winning shot during the famous game. Both he and Monika received top academic awards and scholarships. They were co-valedictorians and left their fellow graduates with the advice to use the skills they learned at school to succeed in life.

*"Have a workable plan on how to reach your goals.*

After posing for photos, the hall was quickly cleared of chairs and the band set up. Brad was pleased that he and Monika managed to dance beautifully together as dancing had not been a big part of their lives. (Fortunately it had been part of the school curriculum.) It just solidified how perfect they were for each other. He knew that this evening would definitely be a lifelong memory—the climax of their first years together.

As he drove up the Johnsons driveway, Brad was surprised to see his parents' car parked on the side of the road.

Why on earth were his parents here? It was the middle of the work week. Had they planned one of their many surprise parties? Must be a BBQ to welcome him back from his successful trip to the university. There had been many such affairs over the years as the two families celebrated their children's victories. He parked his car, jumped out, and ran up the sidewalk to the house, rehearsing how to act surprised. He pictured the scene with banners, balloons, and snacks. Maybe even a beer! He sauntered into the house and was confused when no one called out surprise. Instead, his heart stopped.

Monika was sitting alone in the big antique chair. Her face was swollen with tears, eyes bloodshot and her whole body trembling. He stood frozen in the doorway, glancing at the others in the room. Everyone was in tears. Slowly, he came to realize that something terrible had happened. The tension in the room was palpable. Brad ran to Monika and grabbed her hands. He looked over at his parents who were sitting side by side, holding hands, and wearing expressions he had never seen on them before. Next, he looked over at Monika's parents, who were also sitting side by side with tear-stained faces.

Brad tried to clue into what was happening. Monika had said that she had been sick. Did she have a serious illness? Where were Kristie and Mavis? Had something bad happened to either one or both of the girls?

"Monika, for goodness sake, what is going on? Why is everyone so upset?" Brad cried as he slid into the big chair to hold her in his arms.

"Oh, Brad, I'm pregnant!" Monika cried as she burst into a new round of tears.

With that stunning news, Brad leaned back to look in her eyes. In shock, he shouted, "But we used protection!"

Brad took a moment to digest the news. He flashed back to all the times they had driven to the company office to be alone and make love. How did this happen? Other than the first night, they had used condoms. Had one of the condoms been defective? But within weeks of their first time, Monika had gone to the woman's clinic in Kamloops to get a prescription for birth control pills. Had she not followed the directions? How could this be happening to him—to them? He felt anger creeping up. His perfect life, for the first time ever, was being jolted. He looked at Monika closely. Instead of seeing love and devotion, he saw despair.

From across the room, he heard his father's firm voice saying, "Brad, pay attention."

Both sets of parents were staring at them with a gamut of emotions: shock, denial, disappointment, and confusion. Eventually, by mutual consent arrived at through an earlier discussion, Monika's mother, Flo, began.

"The nausea that Monika has been experiencing these past few weeks is not caused by graduation or college anxiety or even the flu. It is caused by morning sickness. Her pregnancy was a huge surprise. It has been confirmed by the doctor so there is no doubt. Needless to say, we are all extremely traumatized by this turn of events. Your futures are forever drastically changed."

Brad's mother, Mary, took over in what was starting to feel like a well-rehearsed conversation.

"You have both been raised in homes surrounded by love and support. We have always been so proud of both of you—your many accomplishments and successes. Everyone was looking forward to the next five years as you proceeded to further your education and start your careers. Celibacy was always part of your plan. We understand that you are in love and that love has a physical side that is compelling. Monika, you were the champion for waiting until marriage, to the point of hosting a club devoted to supporting girls that needed help saying no. Where does that leave those you have helped? What does it say to Mavis and Kristie, who both adore you? If you had decided to take your relationship to the next level, you could have been married and practiced safe birth control until you were ready to start a family." With that, she once again wiped away tears and leaned on Joe's shoulder.

Monika's dad, Doug, took over the conversation. "Obviously, we have had time to digest the information and try to find solutions to this dilemma. Drastic solutions such as adoption or abortion are totally out of the picture." With that profound statement, he sighed deeply and sat back.

Brad and Monika both felt severely chastised and clung even closer to each other. Never had either of them ever been spoken to so crossly by their parents. They braced themselves for what would be a painful discussion.

Flo once again commanded the direction of the conversation. She took a large gulp of water, wiped her face, sighed deeply, and managed to get control of her voice.

"Monika informed us that the first time you had sex was in the car after the big game. Not the best of circumstances. Since then every time you decided to have sex you had to lie to us about where you were. Even a hurried trip to Kamloops to the woman's clinic to get birth control pills. All of this deceitful behavior to hide your secret. We always trusted you two to be truthful." She began to sob. "You behaved like all the low-life couples that sneak around."

"The best course of action will start with a small family wedding in the church. We will contact the Reverend as soon as possible to set a date. It won't be at all like the ceremony we would have planned for you in five years' time. Then in the fall, Brad will, as planned, head for university. Monika will stay here at home and have the baby. She can begin to study accounting through distant education while she minds the baby. That way, in five years, you will both graduate and start your lives together. It is not quite as planned, as you will be separated for months at a time and there will be a new member in the picture."

All the parents nodded their heads in complete agreement with the plan. It was a done deal in their minds.

Monika had been given a head's up about the plan, but Brad had been away and was in no way prepared for the shocking announcement of the pregnancy nor the neat plan for the future.

Brad and Monika turned to each other and, almost tripping over each other's words, blurted out that in no way would they be separated for five years.

"You cannot separate us. Since I saw the way Monika looked at me the first day of preschool, I knew she would be my advocate forever. She is my strength. I need her close to me."

"I need Brad with me every day. Our new intimacy has bonded us even closer than before. It has fortified our commitment. Separation cannot be an option."

Monika, who had had time to consider alternative options, said. "Yes, Brad must continue to go to university, but there is no reason why I can't go with him and study from there instead of here. I can actually postpone my scholarship for a year then get into full time studying next fall."

That is when Brad dropped another bombshell. He had not yet had the opportunity to discuss how he fared at the university.

"There is a problem with that plan. I haven't been able to tell you yet. At the campus, I met the coaches of basketball and soccer. Being on either team requires living in a separate dorm in order to be properly prepared for practices and out-of-town travel. So we cannot live together. Sports will take up all my time."

Breathing hard and trying to come to terms with this new twist, Monika grasped at straws and blurted out, "There is another option. We could both postpone our scholarships for a year, stay here in town, then both go off to study next fall. Our baby will be old enough for daycare so I can attend classes."

"But, Monika, be realistic. The same situation will be there in a year. I will still be in the dorm. We will still be apart. I would have little time to spend with you and our baby. I want to play an active role in our child's life. It does not make for an ideal situation with both of us juggling studying and parenting."

A long, sometimes heated discussion ensued with no real decision being made. Since Monika and Brad were now adults, the parents could not really dictate what they should do. They did not want Brad to postpone his education as he was in great physical shape and was riding high on his amazing athletic reputation.

Monika tensed as she had not yet given any thought to having to get married. Her mind flashed to what she had always imagined their nuptials to be—a gala affair. Now with a quiet, subdued, almost embarrassing occasion, she felt herself overwhelmed by the enormity of the situation.

Brad also reacted with shock as he had not yet realized that marriage was the next logical step. He wondered how he would feel in a minimal ceremony even if it meant pledging his love for Monika.

Further discussion revolved around how to tell the sisters and grandparents and how members of the church, school, and town would react to the shocking news. It was something they had little control over. Once the news hit the social circles, all sorts of versions would be passed along.

The Andrews and Johnsons had been leading members of the community for years. Gossip would be rapid and rampant. People who admired them would be shocked but understanding. Those who had been envious would react with glee and smugness.

Soon, emotionally exhausted, the Andrews left for home while Brad and Monika slipped away to talk in private about their future. They headed for their favourite place in the nearby park.

"How did this happen? We were so careful," cried Brad.

"It was the night of the final game. Remember, our first time together. We didn't use any protection because it was all so spontaneous," lamented Monika.

"What do you think of the plan to not go to university for a year?" questioned Brad. "We do have to make a decision based on what is most important to us, which is staying together."

"I think I could totally forgo university at this point," Monika said. "I can be at home with our child, studying and getting my accounting licence without leaving town. It will take longer, but I can be a stay-at-home mom. We can still have everything we ever wanted, only not quite as planned. The university is only a two-hour drive away. Our parents will support us. We can see each other every weekend."

"Monika, that won't work. Most games are on the weekends and often out of town."

"Oh, I hadn't thought of that. It is so important for us to experience the pregnancy and birth together. How can we possibly be separated?"

Brad remained silent as his mind was also fighting the odds for a win-win solution.

"You know what I'm thinking? Dad always hoped I would take over the business. I think I can run the business and coach all kinds of sports while never leaving town. It is a great town to raise a family." Brad explained. "University will be very different than high school. The best players from every high school in the province will be my competition for a place on the A-team. I would have to live in a segregated dorm with the athletes. The pressure will be huge. If I can't see you every day, I fear my concentration will be compromised. I need to be with you every day."

They stared at each other, wondering what to do next. Staying together in the same town as man and wife was essential. Beginning a career was negotiable. After another hour of discussion, that they had made a life-changing decision. They decided not to postpone the scholarships, but to give them back.

Before they could be influenced to change their minds, they went to the school to see the members of the scholarship committee and renounce their scholarships.

Because it was summer break, only a skeleton staff remained at the school. There were end-of-the-year loose ends to tidy up and plans for the following year to be scheduled.

When they arrived, they were greeted by the secretary who informed them that Mr. Setters and Ms. McIntyre would be available first thing in the morning. A meeting was set for 8:30.

For the rest of the day, the couple wandered around aimlessly. They stopped at a fast-food outlet and bought burgers and fries. Then, using the pay phone at the restaurant, they called their parents to say that they were going to the cabin for the night to continue discussing the future.

Right on time the next morning, they arrived at the school. They were both truly pleased with the result of their discussions at the cabin and were confident as they arrived at the school.

The secretary ushered them into the office where Mr. Setters and Ms McIntyre were waiting with questioning expressions.

Holding hands and exhaling a deep breath, Brad and Monika said in well-rehearsed unison, "We have decided to hand in our scholarships and stay in town." Silence followed.

"Are you two sure? This is a life-changing decision. If you feel you are not ready to go to university, you can postpone the scholarships. You are the best students this school has seen in a long time. Throwing away promising careers is not a decision to be made lightly," argued Ms. McIntyre.

Mr. Setters was also confused. In all his years, he had never seen such a dramatic turn of events.

"Have you two discussed this with your parents? They have always been supportive of you. They must be reeling with this information."

Monika and Brad exchanged hooded looks.

"Oh my, you haven't told them have you? You know they would not approve! My goodness, let's phone them to come immediately and find out what is behind this new plan."

"No," said Brad. Monika nodded her support. "This is only about us. We are adults and do not need our parents' blessing or consent to make this decision. Twice now, we have overheard our parents making remarks about their hopes for early retirement. It will be nearly another ten years before Mavis and Kristie are finished university. None of the four of us were interested in carrying on either the scrap yard or accounting businesses so they were thinking of selling the business in ten years. Those conversations made me, us, rethink the future. I figured I would do five years of university then graduate as a professional athlete or a PE teacher and coach. But I started looking intensely at Coach Palmer and wondered, "Is that my destiny? Qualify as a professional athlete, get injured, then spend my years as a high school coach? Instead, if I take over Dad's business, I have the freedom to be more in control of my life. By doing this, I can let my parents semi-retire while they teach me the business, then they'll be free to do what they want."

Monika then spoke up. "I have worked for Mom and Dad over the past summers and am quite eager to learn the business by distant education, and they could take me on as an intern. We are very happy about our decisions and anxious to start out new lives right here in Deer Lake."

Mr. Setters and Ms. McIntyre were not about to give up easily and continued to remind them that they could postpone going to university. Nothing made the two teens waver from their decision. Reluctantly, the teachers gave them the papers to sign to revoke their scholarships.

As Monika and Brad left the office, Coach Bruce Palmer walked in and asked if Mr. Setters had a few moments for him. *Well,* Mr. Setters thought, *it's been a shocking day already. What else could happen?*

"I just saw Monika and Brad leaving. They looked absolutely as happy as clams. What's happened?" asked Bruce.

"Brad and Monika are not going to university. They have returned their scholarships and are staying in Deer Lake," replied Mr. Setters.

"What? What? He's a natural athlete. What happens now? Why didn't he postpone it for a year? What?"

"Ms. McIntyre and I tried everything we could, but they were adamant. Don't know what could have happened to precipitate such a dramatic change. Anyway, what can I do for you before Ms. McIntyre and I reassign the scholarships."

"As it turns out, I have some news of my own. I've been head coach here for five years. The last years have been exceptional. As you know, we won the Provincial Championship for the last three years. It was a squeaker this year. Phil was a bit off his game, so I was happy when I saw Brad intercept the ball and make that final goal. You may not be aware that last year after the win, I was approached by a coaching head hunter and asked to submit a resume for an assistant coaching job at a university. I turned it down because I wanted to keep working with the winning team. I was also in a relationship and did not want to risk it. This year after the game, I was offered the job. My partner has left and I have only a few more years where promotion is possible. So I am here to let you be the first to know. I am resigning and moving on," said Bruce.

Bruce and Mr. Setters reminisced and chatted for nearly an hour. When the phone rang, Mr. Setters shook hands with Bruce and wished him the best of luck at the college. He wasn't surprised to hear a very outraged Joe Andrew on the line.

"John what in heaven's name were you thinking? I demand to know why you accepted Brad's scholarship without consulting Mary and me. What kind of incompetence is that? I always respected you as a professional but this is outrageous!"

"Now Joe, calm down. Brad is an adult and free to make his own decisions. His choice to stay in town is his to make."

The connection was abruptly ended.

Now he had to get to work. He and Ms. McIntyre had already agreed on to whom the returned scholarships would go. He needed to deal with that before starting the process to replace Coach Palmer.

\*\*\*

Phil Albright was sitting outside the principal's office totally confused. Graduation was over so really there was no reason for him to be summoned here. He quickly stood up when the outer door opened and Mandy Fleming entered. They looked at each other and simultaneously asked, "Why are we here?" and answered the same way: "I don't know."

Mandy volunteered her news. "I have been accepted into the RN training and have received a student loan. I have a place to stay near the campus and a part-time job lined up. So I should be able to realize my dream to be a nurse."

"Good for you, Mandy. You deserve a chance at success. I also snagged a small bursary and a loan. I'm sharing a dorm room with Martin Brown in a complex reserved for sports students. I also got really good news from my father. When my Grandma died, she left a five-thousand-dollar bond for me to put towards an education. Dad never told me about it because he wanted to me to prove I wanted an education and was willing to work for it," said Phil. "It really shocked me. I never thought he cared about my education. Also, all the times we were broke, he never touched that money. Wow, guess he does love me in his own way."

Just then, the door opened again and Ms. McIntyre entered the waiting room. She nodded at them and lightly knocked on the office door before walking into the principal's office. Phil and Mandy exchanged confused glances. Ms. McIntyre was head of the scholarship committee. They could hear a muted conversation and some laughter. The door opened, and Phil was ushered into the inner office.

Principal Setters greeted Phil and asked him to sit down.

Ms. McIntyre began. "You seem puzzled as to why you were called to this meeting. I guess the town grapevine isn't as strong as I have always believed."

Phil continued to look anxious. Was he about to lose a bursary or loan?

Mr. Setters interjected. "We have some astounding news for you, Phil. It seems that Brad Andrew has returned his scholarship and is giving up his place at the university. He is staying in Deer Lake to take over the family business."

Ms. McIntyre took over at that point. "As a result of his decision the scholarship passes on to you and will be forwarded to the university as soon as your enrolment is confirmed. That is, if you chose to accept it."

"Congratulations, young man. Your future is much more secure with this windfall," added the principal.

Phil was in a state of shock. What had Mr. Setters just said? Brad was not going to university? What did it mean? Phil was getting his scholarship? He felt his hand shake, followed by his whole body. His face was flushed. He ran his fingers through his hair and shook his head as if to find some meaning. Could his luck be changing for the better? Would his struggles be lessened? When he was able to speak, he muttered, "I cannot tell you how much this means to me. I am no longer in second place, and with this, I am free from money worries. Thank you both for this, I will not let you down. Matter of fact, I will be back in five years asking for a reference."

With that, he stood on shaky legs, shook hands with both of them, and left the room in a daze. He barely nodded at Mandy.

Mandy tried to analyze the shocked look on Phil's face as he walked by. She began to fear that he had been given bad news, which meant she may also receive the same.

After a few moments that seemed like forever, Ms.McIntyre opened the door and invited Mandy into the office.

Ms.McIntyre began by asking if she had heard any news about Monika Johnson. Mandy and Monika had been best friends since grade one, so she was aware of the dramatic news about Monika.

Ms.McIntyre began again. "Well, Monika, instead of postponing her scholarship, is returning it because she and Brad will be staying in town."

Ms.McIntyre gave Mandy a minute to gather her thoughts before she stunned her with the other piece of news.

"Mandy, because Monika is returning her scholarship, the award goes to you."

Principal Setters spoke. "Congratulations, Mandy. Your career and future are now much more certain."

Mandy left the office in the same stunned manner that Phil had. She hurried home to share the news with her family. A whole mood of celebration filled the house.

"Mandy, that is such good news. You won't have to work so many hours, leaving you time to study and enjoy some leisure," exclaimed her mom. "As soon as your dad gets home, we're all going out for dinner, at a restaurant, not a fast-food place."

Mandy, her mom, and her sister had a group hug full of tears of joy.

By contrast, Phil immediately went to pick up a case of beer and look for Debbie. This news needed a celebration. Lately, it had been harder to find her. He could hardly wait to tell her the news.

"Debbie, are you home?" Phil yelled as he let himself into the apartment.

"What the heck got into you?" said Debbie as she walked out of her room yawning.

"You will never guess. Brad gave up his scholarship, and I was just awarded it!" Phil could hardly contain himself as he cracked open a beer for each of them. "He is finally out of my life forever. I won't see him on campus, I won't see him on the playing field, and I won't see him here because I am never coming back!"

"Did Monika give up her award as well?" asked an excited Debbie.

"I bet she did because Mandy was next to see the committee bigwigs when I left."

"Oh my God, then the rumors are true. She's pregnant!"

"What? That means Brad will be a daddy not a super star! I wonder what he'll do if he doesn't go to university. Will he work for his dad in the scrap yard, getting dirty and wearing work clothes, pulling cars out of ditches? Maybe he just needs to stay where he's a big fish in the little pond of Deer Lake instead of a national athlete. Always with the cute moonstruck Monika by his side."

"We need to celebrate. I have to stay in town but am going to love seeing the great Monika get fat and carrying around a slobbering, bawling baby!"

For four years, they had both resented Brad and Monika and were happy now that they were no longer the golden couple.

\*\*\*

It was with mixed feelings that Joe and Mary accepted Brad's decision. In fact, part of them had always hoped that Brad and Kristie would take over the business someday. The education fund money would be used to upgrade the facility and Joe could start to take the odd day off.

Brad, who had spent a lot of time at the family business, would now be given more responsibilities. His dad would teach him all the skills of the trade, including how to deal with safety issues and legal and bureaucratic paperwork.

Joe and Brad went to Harry Nichols, their lawyer, to change the business ownership to include Brad. On the advice of the lawyer, the two men took out life insurance and Power of Attorney on each other.

Joe gave his head a shake. He had a fleeting thought that Brad was very happy with the turn of events. Was he afraid to go to university where he would not be the best at everything? Never mind. Things are working out just great!

Meanwhile, Flo and Monika were making wedding preparations. The first step was to visit Reverend Archie Simpson.

"Good morning, ladies," the Reverend greeted them. "I must say, I was very surprised to receive your request for a meeting. You seemed very upset on the phone. Please come into my office."

The Reverend, Flo, and Monika entered the rather cluttered office. Archie quickly rearranged the papers on his desk, ran his fingers through his thinning hair, and offered the ladies a beverage. They both declined.

"Okay, Flo, obviously something is amiss. There is nothing so earth shattering that our Lord cannot help us cope with it, be it illness or death."

Flo, with tears welling in her eyes, saw no other way to open the discussion than to be blunt. Adjusting her skirt and re-crossing her legs, she blurted out, "Monika is pregnant. She and Brad need to be married quickly."

"What did you say? Pregnant? I'm shocked at this news. Monika, you chaired the group supporting celibacy for teens. You and Brad were able to resist temptation—a perfect example of an honourable relationship. Oh dear, oh dear. Let me check my calendar for available dates."

Monika, feeling chastised, began to sob as she realized once again how many people she had let down. She sat rigidly, avoiding eye contact with her mother.

"According to my calendar, we can have the ceremony the first week of September. Will that give you enough time to make arrangements?"

"Yes," Flo replied. "From the altar, we will adjourn to the community room for a small reception. We have very few relatives who are able to attend. Most of our friends are also friends of the Andrews so there will be less than fifty people invited."

"Of course, Brad and Monika will have to take marriage preparation lessons starting immediately. Here, I can give you the workbooks now."

The Reverend stood up and began to usher the ladies out. He stopped and said, "Be sure to give me the names of the two witnesses as soon as possible. Also, I will need the names of the psalms and songs you would like to hear."

Once back in the car, they decided to head straight home. Mary Andrew was expected at two o'clock to discuss the date, invitation list, catering, and the colour theme for wardrobe and decorations.

A modest wedding was planned for September 8 after the Labour Day weekend. Flo, Mary, and Monika made a comprehensive checklist of what needed doing in order to make the day wonderful despite the short timeline. First, they secured the church and adjoining hall as a venue. The Ladies Auxiliary of the church was quick to assist since Flo and Mary had been active members for years. They arranged for the organist, DJ, photographer, and florist, who were all church members. They would also cater the dinner and help with set up and take down. Flo, Mary, Monika Mavis, and Kristie set up a work centre to hand-write the few invitations and place cards and assemble the table centrepieces.

The day of the wedding was a warm, sunny fall day. The church and adjoining hall were resplendent in fall colours of orange and yellow. Flo and Mary, wearing dresses in yellow and orange respectively, were seated. Brad and his father were waiting at the altar wearing dark suits with orange boutonnieres. A large vase of fall flowers was on the altar. The Reverend entered to stand by the podium as the organist began to play the wedding march. First Mavis and Kristie came down the aisle wearing knee length dresses that had a pattern of yellow and orange. Monika was beaming as she leaned on her father's arm. Her plain white sheath barely showed her pregnancy. She had orange and yellow ribbons flowing from the ringlets in her hair. When she looked up and saw Brad waiting for her, she nearly exploded with happiness.

Reverend Simpson waited until everyone was settled before he began the ceremony. Once he explained the sanctity of the wedding vows, he turned to the beaming couple and invited Brad to express his vows.

With tear filled eyes and a raspy voice Brad proclaimed, "Monika, you have always been my inspiration and supporter, the force behind my life. I will be by your side forever. You complete me."

Reverend nodded to Monika.

"Brad I knew from the beginning I would be with you forever. We are blessed with our love and family. You are my soul mate."

Reverend then instructed them to exchange rings and announced that they may kiss.

Once the Reverend had introduced them as man and wife, they walked out of the church into the courtyard for the family photos. All the different hues of orange and yellow and the maple trees in the background, made for a very colourful scene. The decorations in the hall continued the theme. Once the dinner was done, the bride and groom thanked their parents and sisters for the support they had received.

Then the dancing started. Once again, he and Monika danced flawlessly together. Kristie danced every dance with the fathers. The many years of lessons made her able to follow the waltz, fox trot, and polka with ease. She and Mavis danced to the more modern tunes. Soon the happy couple left for a short honeymoon at the cabin.

When Brad and Monika returned from their honeymoon, they moved into Monika's bedroom. Every morning Brad left for work at the Apex Auto Wreckers and Monika worked on the assignments leading towards her CPA degree. It was a temporary arrangement that suited everyone but Mavis, who was upset at not being able to move into the bigger bedroom.

The town gossip had run its course and most people were onto other news.

Flo, Mary and Monika spent many hours with a realtor looking to find an affordable home for the new family. Once they had visited a dozen possibilities, they made a short list of three homes. Then Joe, Doug and Brad reviewed their choices. It was unanimous decision to purchase a small older home near the centre of town.

Monika threw herself into preparations for the arrival of the baby. She thoroughly cleaned and painted their home. The smaller bedroom was decorated as the nursery with a rainbow theme. Joe and Doug assembled a crib and changing table. Flo and Mary knitted and sewed colourful curtains, quilts and baby outfits. By the end of October they had moved into their partially furnished home.

Brad was working long hours at the business. During the winter months he had qualified for an enhanced driver's licence so that he could operate the tow truck, fork lift and the heavy industrial equipment.

Brad was surprised when he realized that he was actually enjoying his new career. He loved leaving the job and going home to Monika. She often surprised him with a new recipe as she learned how to use all the kitchen appliances and gadgets they had received as wedding gifts.

The pregnancy was progressing normally. Her shape was slowly changing and her glow was beautiful. Monika was so happy with her new life.

As fall progressed, they spent the weekends starting to tame the wild overgrown garden. Some old trees would have to be removed and the vegetable garden resurrected. The wooden fence also would need rebuilding in the near future.

Soon it was time to prepare for their first Christmas in their home. Mavis and Kristie helped them decorate the house with colourful seasonal items. Monika baked all the cookies that were traditional at the Johnson's home.

Joe and Mary hosted the traditional Christmas dinner. A week later, Flo and Doug hosted the annual New Year's Eve celebration at the Lake, complete with fireworks and lots of food.

The winter months sped by with Brad keeping busy pulling poorly tired cars out of the snow banks and ditches. Some weekends were still spent at the Lake with ice fishing, sledding and a camp fire.

# CHAPTER 3

# 1991-1995

The months continued to speed by and on March 1, 1991, Monika's labour began. Brad grabbed the 'Ready To Go' bag and rushed her to the hospital. Doctor Tait examined her and assured them both that all was well but it may be a few hours yet.

Brad tried to relax. He went to the pay phone to alert both sets of parents. Soon the waiting room was crowded with Flo, Doug, Mary, Doug, Mavis and Kristie. Nervous excitement filled the waiting room. The prenatal classes had prepared Monika for the birthing process. Brad was with her for the twelve hours that it took to deliver Robert Bradley Andrew, who weighed in at a healthy six pounds and measured twenty one inches in length. He aced the APAP examination. His entry into the world was accompanied by very loud vocal protest.

Young Bobby proved to be a healthy contented baby. Monika flourished as a mother, attending Lamaze lessons and joining Mother and Tot Social Group that offered support for many mothers. They could share the joys and concerns of parenting.

As soon as Brad finished his job, he showered at the office and hurried home. He gave Monika a hug and kiss but hurried immediately to see Bobby, hoping he was awake.

When spring arrived, Doug, Joe and Brad built a deck off the kitchen door and planted a tree in honour of Bobby's birth.

Kristie and Mavis often came over to spend time with Bobby. They took him for walks in the buggy and sang and read to him. They often babysat so that the parents could have a bit of time to themselves.

Flo and Mary continued to make new clothes to accommodate Bobby's growth spurts.

Monika had done well on her first semester. She was able to take the summer off to work in the office, relieving her parents. Brad was doing well enough at the yard to allow his parents a few days off. Both couples headed to the cabins at the lake.

Everything was going so well. Neither of them regretted not to university. Brad was establishing himself as business man in the town by joining Chamber of Commerce and Rotary. He was coaching men's basketball as well.

Monika was active in the church groups and was teaching toddlers to swim.

Summer began with a lavish family July 1$^{st}$ picnic. Everyone showed up proudly wearing red and white. Streamers, flags and balloons adorned the newly spruced up yard. Flo arrived with a plate of appetizers reflecting the colour theme, with red tomatoes, radishes and white apple slices, coconut and parsnips. Mary contributed a dessert of red jelly, vanilla ice cream and maple leaf shaped cookies with red sprinkles.

The men were busy at the BBQ and the aunts were vying for Bobby's attention. Even the recently widowed neighbour, Ralph Cornwallis, arrived with red and white wine, and cranberry and white grape juice.

Games of lawn darts, soccer and badminton were played. Bobby was never alone and managed to be the center of attention by displaying his new found skill of rolling over.

By the time the celebration was over and the clean-up was complete, an exhausted Brad and Monika went to bed, very happy with their life.

Summer was soon over. Brad and Monika celebrated their first anniversary with a trip to Kamloops.

Kristie and Mavis left for university. Bobby learned to crawl and to pull himself up on furniture.

Fall turned into winter and it was Bobby's first Christmas. A family conference decided to have the gift opening at Bobby's but the other celebrations would be held at the traditional places. It was also decided that a ten month old child did not need a dozen gifts as he would have no idea what it was all about. As a result he received one gift each from the Andrew and Johnson family and from Mom and Dad. No Santa Claus gift. Instead, an education fund was set up with contributions from all.

January 1992 the Andrews went to Mexico for a vacation and the Johnsons to Africa to visit Flo's mother.

For Bobby's first birthday, Monika arranged a play date with the children from the Mother's Support Group. Then on Sunday, after church service, the family had a brunch and birthday cake. Once again, gifts were limited and money placed in his education fund.

The next few years continued to flow as Bobby learned to walk, run and to use more and more words. The two sets of grandparents began taking more time off. Brad hired a part time worker. Monika completed her studies, worked for her parents and taught swimming. Brad was president of the Rotary and much esteemed in town as an astute businessman. He was being groomed by some to enter politics.

\*\*\*

"Deb", called Helen as she entered their apartment. "Why is there a telephone crew here? Is there a problem with our phone?"

"No, Mom, relax. I am having a private line installed. I have been hired as an operator for a call centre and will need a separate line because it will have a 1-800 number. I will also have an answering machine as calls can be made 24-7. This way the house phone won't be busy while I'm working." answered Deb with her well rehearsed response.

The truth was that thanks to lawyer Walter Brown she was establishing a clientele for her escort and massage business.

She was learning how to manage her business. Her client, the banker helped her get a loan, the realtor helped her purchase a small condo as a place to conduct her business and a financial advisor set up her investments.

Deb continued to live at home with her mother who was finally proud of her self sufficient daughter. Helen never quite understood what Deb did but was glad that she was contributing not only money to the household but was often doing chores as well.

\*\*\*

The next three years were marvelous for Phil. He was no longer in Brad's shadow. No one at the university knew anything about him, except that he was there on scholarship. Thanks to Coach Palmer, his skill level was A-team worthy.

He wondered why he was being called to the Dean's office as he knocked on the door and entered when invited.

The Dean was seated behind a large mahogany desk. He was wearing the varsity jacket and tie over a crisp white shirt. He had a very serious look on his face as he directed Phil to take a seat.

"Phil, it has been brought to my attention that you have a very high profile here at the campus. Such a position comes with certain behavioural expectations. Your athletic prowess is an asset. With the help of a tutor, your grades are acceptable. As you know, your scholarship defines not only your game strength and course grades but also your conduct."

"Yes, I am well aware of the terms of my scholarship. I sense there is an issue about one of the three areas," said Phil as a feeling of dread came over him.

"Yes, Phil. We have received complaints from two students about behaviour that appears to be very sexist and demeaning. Both of the students are willing to accept an apology at this time. However, for every one that lodges a formal complaint, it has been my experience that there are many unreported."

Phil felt a wave of panic overwhelm him. Could he lose everything he had worked so hard for?

"Dean Lapoint, I am so sorry and embarrassed. I have been feeling so successful and happy lately that I may have stepped out of line. Please let me apologize contritely to the accusers. I will absolutely not let anything like this happen again," he cried.

"Your coaches and I, along with Human Resources, have decided that the complaints are based on inappropriate comments not actions. It seems both complaints happened when alcohol was present. We are willing to place you on probation for a month. If there is even a hint of sexist behaviour, you will be suspended."

Phil left the office feeling scared. He was more than halfway through his five years of study. He couldn't screw it up now.

The Dean arranged meetings with the offended students. All involved accepted Phil's sincere apologies. He vowed to watch his behaviour. The first step was to stop going to parties that involved liquor. That was where the breaches had occurred. Drinking was his dad's downfall. He would not repeat history!

CHAPTER 4

# SUMMER 1990

Now that he had graduated from Rangeland High School, José Lopez was deep in thought, reviewing his life's story. Years ago in the early 1970s, his parents, Pedro and Maria Lopez, had legally immigrated to Rangeland, B.C., full of love and dreams of a better life. Rangeland was a small community deep in the heart of cattle country. It was the commercial centre for the ranchers and farmers of the area. After just one year, the dream was closer to a nightmare when the agriculture industry took a huge downturn. They were both hard workers willing to take on any job. But the only jobs available were part time, low paying, and seasonal. With both of them working anywhere they could, they still barely made ends meet. They used the food bank, soup kitchens, and the church charity to survive. When Maria became pregnant and had to cut back her hours even more, Pedro became depressed. One day, he just vanished.

Maria was left alone, devastated and scared. The woman's auxiliary of the church stepped in to help. She was given a small living space in the church basement in return for light duties. When it was time to deliver, the women once again were there for her to welcome her son José into the world.

Maria and another single mom moved into a small two bedroom home owned by the church. They shared expenses and babysat for one another while working and taking courses that would lead to marketable skills in the field of caring for elderly persons. Four years and many different roommates later, Maria graduated and applied for positions at every extended care facility in the area.

Maria was hired by a Government Senior's Care Home. Because of her work skills and ethics, she earned a full-time position. The contract came with medical, dental, and pension benefits. It also qualified her to lease a two-bedroom house. Her Canadian dream was finally happening.

She rented out the second bedroom to college students for a small rent in exchange for babysitting.

When José was six, Maria felt that he should have the bedroom to himself instead of sharing a room with her. She quit taking in students but that meant on rare occasions she had to leave him home alone for an hour after school. She lived in fear of him being in danger or of the authorities finding him alone. Fortunately, that never happened.

By the time José was eight, he had started making some money collecting recyclables. He was much loved in the area, and soon neighbours were saving cans and bottles for him and hiring him to mow lawns and shovel snow.

One life changing day, José happened upon a yard sale. He grew intrigued by the culture and soon learned that at the end of the day prices were reduced drastically, sometimes to the point of being free.

José used some of his precious money to buy a bicycle that was in rough shape. He fixed it up and built a small cart to pull behind. He was now in the business of weekend yard sales. Many times at the end of a yard sale, José noticed a man with a truck was also picking over the remains. One day the man approached him.

"Hello young fellow. You are becoming my competition," he said smiling.

"No sir, I only takes the things that are less than $1.00 if I think I can clean them up."

"Well, what do you do with things that you fix up?"

"So far I have just saved them so maybe one day I will have a garage sale."

"Well let's see if we can make a deal. My name is Curtis Middlemass and I own Best Ever Used Items. It is a second hand store down town. What's your name?"

"Sorry Sir, I have to go home now."

"I bet your mom told you to never talk to strangers, especially those with a truck nearby. How about I give you my business card and you ask your mom to phone me. I would like to make a business deal with you. I will buy the items you fix and when you are fifteen, I can hire you to work in my shop."

"I guess that would be okay. My name is José and my mom is Maria."

Maria did phone Curtis and met with him. The result was a ten year business relationship between the two bargain hunters. Curtis became a father like figure as well as a mentor.

A few years later he encouraged José to start taking course to become a paramedic. While working for Curtis and studying, he was building a future for himself. He had little time for sports or friends.

\*\*\*

The future seemed rosy. Maria's work record qualified her for a mortgage. She bought a small house with a basement suite. Remembering her own story, she wanted to rent the suite to a woman who was pregnant and alone. The church office suggested that Maria and José interview Erin Oates. She seemed pleasant and grateful for the opportunity to do a bit of house and yard work in exchange for a reduced rent.

When Erin went into labour, José drove her to the Rangeland Hospital. After a lengthy labour, Erin delivered a healthy baby boy. Maria and José stayed until she was resting. They returned three days later to take Erin and her son James Matthew home. As they were packing her up, a nurse arrived with the discharge papers. Erin read them, signed, and then asked José if he would endorse the form that confirmed she was Erin Oates.

The days and weeks went by in harmony. José would continue to work and take courses. Maria was promoted to shift manager and was making more money. Erin started a part-time job as a waitress and her friend Shelley Burrows babysat Matt.

\*\*\*

Anne started out in life in a happy, loving home in Rangeland. She was the only child of doting parents Natalie and Tomas Novakova, who came to Canada from Poland. In August of 1968, due to the Warsaw Pact, Natalie's sister Tereza and her husband Jakup Cerny along with more than ten thousand other people left

Poland and the Czech Republic for Canada. When the
Novakovas arrived two years later, they were surprised
to discover that Tereza and Jakup had Anglicized
their names. They were now known as Terry and Jake
Black. They seemed to want to minimize their Polish
culture and become as Canadian as possible. In 1972,
Natalie and Tomas had a daughter that they named
Julia Anna Novakova.

Life for Julia came to a sudden stop when her
wonderful parents were killed in a plane crash. The
only last will and testament to be located was nearly
ten years old, written before Julia was born. It left
everything to Natalie's now estranged sister, who soon
took over all the legal paper work necessary to settle
their affairs. She also assumed responsibility for Julia,
even though there was no mention of her in the will.
They quickly Anglicized her name to Anne Novak
when they registered her for school. Within a year,
the aunt and uncle decided that raising a child, even a
mild-tempered one, was not what they wanted. Their
own children were teenagers, and they were looking
forward to empty-nesting, not starting over.

"Anne, come here I need to talk to you," called
Aunt Terry one day.

Anne hurried into the living room and sat close to
her aunt.

"Anne, it is very sad that your parents are dead.
Uncle Jake and I have looked after you for a year. But

now it is time for us to move to the city so your cousins can attend college. We have arranged for you to move into a lovely home so you can stay here in Rangeland instead of having to move to Kamloops with us. It will be better for you as it will be one less change for you to make."

"I don't understand. I want to go with you. No one else is family. Will I live with my best friend Carol and her family?" queried a confused Anne.

"No, even better, you will live with a foster family. These people are like professional parents. They take in children who have no family to look after them."

"But I have you for my family."

"I told you, you cannot come with us. There is no room for you in our new house. A very nice lady will come for you this afternoon so you can meet your new family. I have packed all of your belongings so she won't have to wait. I need to finish packing for the family."

Anne stood transfixed. What was happening? Was her young life being trashed once again? Why did she need a new family? She wanted to cry but didn't know why. Would she go to live with her aunt after they were settled in their new home? She took a deep breath to stop the trembling in her legs.

"Oh, here is the lady now." Anne's aunt opened the door. "Hello, Meredith, come on in. Anne is ready to go with you now. Anne, come over here and meet Ms. Rutherford. She will take you to your nice new home."

"Hello Anne. Do you remember me? I came to visit your aunt here two weeks ago? I see that you are all packed and ready to move. Say goodbye to your Aunt Terry and come with me. I'm happy to take you to your new home. You will live with Mr. and Mrs. Moore while we look for a more permanent place for you. I know you're confused but it will all be fine. Let's get your suitcase and binder and get into the car."

Anne was confused about what was happening. She followed Ms. Rutherford out to her car but felt panicky so turned back towards the house only to see her Aunt Terry had already closed the door.

Anne stopped walking and pulled her hand out of Meredith's. She stood looking first at the closed house door and then at the open car door. She choked back tears as she began to understand what was happening. She started to sob. Meredith bent down to hug her and reassure her that all was fine. She assisted Anne into the car, reached into a bag, and withdrew a cute stuffie for Anne to hug.

Anne's first foster home with the Moore family was across town so she was forced to change schools. It would be her third school in as many years: kindergarten while still with her mom, a second school while with her aunt, and now another place to try and fit in. At first she had her own small room, but a month later, Mr. Moore's daughter from a previous marriage moved into the home. Against the rules of foster care, the girl moved into the bedroom with Anne.

One night, Anne awoke in a fright when she realized the older girl had not only crawled into bed with her but was touching her inappropriately. She jumped out of the bed. Her screams awoke the parents who immediately demanded to know what was troubling her.

"Are you having a nightmare?" asked Mrs. Moore, ready to cuddle Anne.

"No, she came into my bed and was touching me down there!"

"No I wasn't. She's lying."

"What's going on?" asked Mr. Moore as he entered the room.

"Anne's telling lies about me. I can't believe she is so mean," blubbered his daughter.

"No, that's not true!" cried Anne.

"I don't believe you Anne. My daughter has been here a lot when we have had other foster children and has never done anything wrong. We will call Ms. Rutherford at Family Services and have her send you elsewhere." he declared.

No one would listen to her, and she was once again moved. Because she was now labeled a problem child, she was assigned to a stricter, more monitored home. This time, she did not change schools but that was not an asset as the students who lived at that address had the reputation of being tough.

Anne had to learn to assume a different character to match her new position. She had always been aloof, so it was not too difficult to stay the 'quiet' one. Many of the other foster children had serious emotional issues and therefore caused a lot of stress in the home. Survival, she soon learned, meant keeping a low profile at the home and at school.

Two years later, her probation as a difficult child was rescinded. Now nearly fifteen, she was transferred to her third and final home. Since it coincided with the transfer from middle school to high school, she was not the only new student at her school. She actually recognized some students from her previous schools as this was the merging of two other schools.

Her final placement was at the home of Mr. and Mrs. Raeburn. She was the oldest of four foster children in their home and soon took on the role of big sister. She became invaluable to the Raeburns, who paid her to babysit and help with homework assignments.

Before long, Anne had established a comfortable routine. She would walk the seven year old twins Zoe and Zack and the six year old boy Seth home from school. She would listen to their accounts of the school day. Once home, they would all enjoy a snack with Mrs. Raeburn. They would spend an hour playing in the backyard or in the den before starting any homework assignments. After dinner, the twins cleared the table while Anne supervised Seth's exercise routine—necessary to help strengthen his muscles weakened by hypotonia, also known as floppy infant syndrome.

It was a win-win deal. For the first time in her life, Anne had a little spending money. She quickly started a bank account. Anne continued to remain aloof at school to concentrate on studying and taking the maximum number of courses.

At age eighteen, she was about to graduate from high school and, unfortunately, from the system. She would soon be aged out. Policies for free tuition at some educational faculties were few and far between. Fortunately, Anne's school grades qualified her for a small bursary.

Shortly before graduating, Anne was summoned to the office of Ms. Lisa Chow, the school counselor.

Lisa had been guiding parentless students for over twenty years. She had not had an easy life so had empathy for those without a family. Lisa understood how facing the world was a challenge for every teen, but one without a network had even more obstacles. Anne would soon be let loose, unprepared for the world. Thankfully, the Raeburns had been her last home and that was a blessing.

Ms. Chow ushered Anne into the office.

"Good morning, Anne. Please have a seat. I assume, like most graduates, you're feeling a gamut of emotions."

"Yes, I am. It's one more big change in my life. I'm not totally sure about what comes next."

"Absolutely. I'm here today to help you move from school and foster care to being on your own. Anne, I totally understand that the current system lacks a lot of support. This is what I have done in the past for students in your unenviable position. You can take a room in Mama Murphy's Rooming House. You can sign up for a course at the college. The shortest program is as a practical nursing program. You definitely have the right personality for the career with your history of working with Seth. The best news is that most of it can be done through distant education. You will need to do practicum hours as well as in-class or online studies. I suggest you take a part-time job somewhere. It gives you flexible hours, an income to pay Mama for a room, and money to buy food and other essentials."

Someone rapped lightly at the door and entered the room. Anne recognized her as Ms. Kathy Preston, the latest social worker assigned to her case.

"Anne, I have information for you. You are eligible for a small allowance from the government program as long as you are studying. I believe that Ms. Chow will be giving you advice to help you chose a career. I must say, it has been a pleasure working with you and

I will continue to be your go-to-person. Feel free to call me if you ever need advice or guidance. Good luck."

She shook Anne's hand and left a manila folder with Ms. Chow. Anne was given the envelope at the end of her meeting. When she got home, she placed it with all her school records such as report cards, assignments she was proud of, and other little mementos. She did not open it.

Mrs. Raeburn attended her graduation ceremony, which was nice as all the other graduates had families cheering for them. There was one lone voice along with a few applauding teachers as she took her turn across the stage. Mrs. Raeburn told Anne she could stay with them until her nineteenth birthday in two months, then funding for her would cease. The monthly stipend from the government would then be paid directly to Anne.

"Now what happens to me?" sighed Anne.

\*\*\*

When Anne returned home that day, she went to the college website and learned that the practical nursing program would take seventy-five weeks if she studied full time, but the health care assistant program would take only thirty weeks. She made an appointment with the college counselor to get guidance. There she was told that her hours could be flexible, and she could do a lot of the book learning on her own. Practicum hours could be arranged to fit her schedule. Her future income would be reflected by the program. She was willing to commit to the longer program if it meant she could earn an income that would allow her to be independent.

Once her schooling was arranged, Anne visited Mama Murphy's Rooming House and learned there were three bedrooms available for rent. The largest room had four twin beds with foot lockers and a full bathroom. The second room had two beds, the third had a single bed and a lock on the door. The tenants in the second and third rooms shared a full bathroom. There was a small kitchen with a fridge, microwave, and toaster oven, and a third bathroom with just a toilet and sink.

The weekly rent varied according to which room you were in and if you were willing to do some of the cleaning.

Knowing her limited resources, Anne chose to share the room with four beds and to reduce her rent by cleaning the common rooms. Having lived in foster care for years, she had learned to never leave valuables around. Even locked foot lockers offered no guarantee of securing valuables. Anne decided to use her backpack as a place to put everything. Her daily toiletries were in a small bag in her pack as was any cash that she had. To cover the rest of the costs, Anne found a waitressing job at a diner to make a few extra dollars. The diner owner quickly became aware of her work ethic, people skills, and commitment. Since the owner also managed a dining room, he asked her to switch jobs. Before long, she was earning not only higher wages but also generous tips. Her small bank balance started to grow.

The next two and a half years were a blur. She managed to get by on less than six hours of sleep as her days were busy with cleaning the rooming house, waiting tables, studying, and doing practicum hours. Because both jobs required a uniform, she did not have to buy a wardrobe. She remained in the big room as she watched her roommates change nearly weekly. She was too busy to form any lasting friendships with them, but about once a week, she and Mama Murphy would sit and chat over a cup of tea. They both looked forward to these meetings as they were both loners. Anne learned that Mama and Ms. Chow had not only been friends for years, but they often went on holidays together.

Lisa and Mama had lived together for a while until the parents of some students declared that as a lesbian, Lisa would not be able to give good advice to the students. There were also ugly stories going around that the only reason she was hired in the first place was not for her skills but because she was a visible minority and satisfied the popular reverse discrimination policy.

For the next two years, Anne continued to live her solitary life until her graduation from the practical nursing program. This time, there was nobody at the ceremony to cheer for her.

However, once again reality burst her balloon. There were no full-time positions available for practical nurses. The best she could do was register as on call with various facilities. So she had to remain waitressing and living at the rooming house.

It took another year before she was able to get two permanent part-time jobs, one at a long term care facility and one at the hospital recovery room.

Shortly after Anne got settled with her new jobs, Mama Murphy gave notice that the rooming house had sold and Anne would have to find alternate accommodations. She found a small studio apartment close to the hospital. The bad news was that the apartment required two months' rent plus a damage deposit up front. That withdrawal seriously depleted her bank account.

From the Best Ever Used Items second-hand store, Anne purchased a futon, kitchen table with two chairs, and a small dresser. These expenses left her with a nearly empty bank account. But for the first time since she was very young, she had her own space. She was soon popular at both jobs. Because she was so used to being on the go eighteen hours a day, she took on a few side jobs as well, going to private homes to administer care, such as changing dressings or bathing a patient.

\*\*\*

To celebrate Matt's third birthday, Erin planned a picnic in the park. Maria, José, Shelley, and Sean Jackson, Erin's new boyfriend, were all there. Shelley and Erin set up the food and gifts at the table. After the gifts were opened and the food consumed, Erin hugged and kissed Matt with more affection than usual, then suggested José and Maria take him to the other end of the park to play with his new Frisbee while she and Sean cleared the picnic table. Matt loved the thrill of trying to catch and throw the Frisbee. The three of them were having a great time when Shelley showed up to join them.

"Hi guys, you look like you're having fun. Erin and Sean are having a big fight so I thought I would come and join you."

Maria briefly wondered if Erin was once again choosing the wrong kind of man for a partner. But she set her worries aside as the four of them continued to play for another fifteen minutes until Matt was exhausted. They returned to the picnic table to find the remnants of the party still on the table, but Sean and Erin were gone. José drove his car closer to the picnic table so Maria and Shelley could pack up the gifts and they could head back to the house. They drove home in silence, each lost in their own thoughts.

Sean's car was not at the house, so they called for Erin to come out. When there was no response, Shelley noticed the door was open so she entered in, still calling for Erin. She walked through the kitchen area and into the bathroom. There was no sign of Erin, so she continued into the bedroom. The closet and dresser were empty. It appeared as though Erin had moved out.

In a daze, Shelley looked around as if to confirm what she saw. That is when she noticed papers on the bed. She went back outside carrying the papers to tell Maria and José what she had discovered. She handed the papers to José.

"Oh, good, here is a note from her." After quickly reading it, José exclaimed, "Oh no! How could she do this?" Maria and Shelley were anxious to know the contents of the note. He handed it to them to read together. Both had similar reactions.

> *Dear Shelley and José,*
>
> *I am pregnant. Sean does not want to raise another man's son as well as his own child, so we are leaving. Shelley,*

> *why don't you move into the suite and*
> *continue to care for Matt? I have left you*
> *some money and all the important docu-*
> *ments. – Erin*

Matt, sensing tension, started to whine for his mom. He ran into the apartment looking for her. Before long, he was in a full bout of sobs, calling "I want my mommy. Where is my mommy?"

The others followed him into the bedroom where he was on the bed punching the pillow and calling for his mommy.

Maria went towards Matt to comfort him but suddenly felt weak, she had trouble breathing and broke out in a cold sweat. Feeling lightheaded and nauseous, she went to sit on the bed to catch her breath. Instead, she fell onto the bed close to Matt.

José was frantically calling her name. Then his first aid training kicked in and he began chest comprehensions.

He checked her breathing and pulse and yelled. "Shelley, quick call 911 and tell them we have a heart attack patient."

Shelley sprang into action to make the call, then went over to comfort Matt who was crying hysterically. The emotions of the day were confusing him. He had gone from a happy celebration in the park to realizing that something was amiss not only with his mother but now with everyone else.

The paramedics arrived and asked about Maria's age and any medications or recent heart problems. They quickly assessed the situation and transported her to the hospital where the staff began working on her immediately. She was placed in ICU. José stayed with her until she had stabilized then rushed home to check on Matt and Shelley.

Shelley greeted him with the other papers Erin had left behind. "You better look at these papers."

José scanned the documents: Matt's birth certificate, immunization papers, and SIN papers. But what left him breathless were the hospital birth registration papers. It stated the father was José Lopez!

What? He hadn't even met Erin until after she was pregnant. He never touched her. How could this be? He looked again and recognized his signature at the bottom. He studied the paper a bit more. The truth hit him like a ton of bricks. That was the paper she asked him to sign verifying her identity at the hospital.

It took him a moment to digest the news that Erin had put his name down as Matt's father. His shock turned to anger. He turned to Shelley.

"What did you know about this?" he demanded. "She must have told you what she was planning! Are you a part of this? How long has she been planning this?"

Shelley reacted as if she had been slapped. "How dare you accuse me of having any part in this? I've only known Erin for two years, and until she met Sean, she was a good mother and friend."

José took a deep breath, shook his head, and fought back tears. The anger quickly dissipated and was replaced by confusion as he realized he had no right to accuse Shelley of conspiring with Erin. "Shelley, I'm so sorry. There is too much happening. I need you to help me with mom and Matt and what to do. Do you know where they might have gone?"

"I have no idea, and I most definitely do not want to be a mother to my friend's kid. She has left some money and food so I will look after him until you find out what's going on with Maria."

José visited his mother daily, often bringing Matt with him. The poor boy still cried every day for his mom, but knew he was loved by José, Maria, and Shelley.

Maria continued to recover in the hospital for the next month. She soon became a staff favourite because she was so cooperative, friendly, and eager to get better. Maria was especially fond of one practical nurse that cared for her. Anne Novak was always empathetic and cheerful. She was often in the room when José and Matt came to visit. Sometimes José and Anne would find themselves looking at each other. José had never had a girlfriend so did not quite know if she was just being a competent nurse or if she was being friendly. Likewise, Anne had never had a boyfriend. She felt an attraction to José, but warned herself to stay aloof. After all, he did have a son, which meant he likely had a partner.

One day while Anne was working, Maria engaged her in conversation, mentioning that José was her son and Matt was a family friend. Then Maria asked Anne about her relationship status. Anne blushed and wondered about the motive of Maria's conversation.

Maria was sent home to recover. Shelley was still in the suite and was able to pay some rent as she had begun babysitting another four-year-old boy named Chad. She was willing to mind Matt when he was not in preschool but drew the line at doing any nursing jobs.

José then approached Anne and explained that because he was on twelve hour shifts at the Fire Hall and was still doing some hours at the Best Ever Used Items store, he needed someone to come to the house for a couple of hours three days a week to mind Maria. Anne was only too happy to take on the extra job and, she secretly had to admit, she wanted to stay in touch not only with Maria, but with José and Matt as well— especially now that she knew José was not married. Mysteriously, she was beginning to have feelings that confused her.

Anne's visits to the house to provide home care for Maria continued for a few weeks. It seemed that José would often be there for a few minutes when she arrived. Some days, he would come home a little early and invite her to stay for coffee. It was obvious to Maria and Shelley, if not to José and Anne, that there was chemistry between the two.

Maria appeared to be recovering but eventually suffered another attack. Despite all efforts by the paramedics and the ER staff, she passed away.

A small ceremony was held at the church. José was feeling sad and alone until he saw Anne in the church. Matt saw Anne and ran up to her for a hug. The three of them had spent so much time together over the past few months that they were beginning to feel like a family.

A few days after the service, José went to the safe in his mom's room and was shocked at what he found. Not only was the little house nearly mortgage-free, but it was in his name as well. (That was the secret paper she made him sign on his eighteenth birthday. He had to learn to read papers before signing them!) Also, there was a small life insurance policy from the union plus a modest savings account. What a shame that Maria had worked so hard but passed away before she could enjoy the rewards. Once over the shock, José realized that he was in a good position financially. He could pay off his student loans and make some badly needed repairs on the house.

He was interrupted by a knocking on the door. Assuming it was people offering condolences, he was surprised to see Shelley there.

"Good morning, Shelley. I just made coffee and opened a package of cookies. Come on in. What's up? Where's Matt?"

"No thanks. Matt and Chad are watching cartoons. I have something I need to discuss with you. I'm going to move in with Chad's mother and register for night classes to earn my GED. So I'm giving you notice." Then she dropped another bombshell. "I was going to surrender Matt to social services but thought I'd ask you first what you want to do."

José was in a state of shock. He loved Matt and couldn't imagine life without him. "Please don't do anything so drastic yet. Matt has been part of the family since he was born. He considers us his parents. I am down legally as his father. I cannot deal with this situation until I seek legal advice."

José consulted Miguel Gonzales, a lawyer he knew through the church, and asked for advice.

"It looks to me that you have two legal choices, both of which will have a moral and emotional toll. Since you are legally down as the father, you can do nothing but continue to take care of him. Or you can involve child services, which means you will probably have to pay child support even if he is in the foster program," advised Miguel. "A DNA test will can be arranged to prove you are not the biological father and that may have an impact on the decision."

Reeling from this new situation, José wandered aimlessly around the park. He was surprised to see Anne Novak also wandering. They sat down together on a bench in silence for a while.

Before long, José unburdened his horrible dilemma to Anne. He had less than a week to decide if he should keep Matt or call social services.

In a flash, Anne was screaming at him and pounding his chest, shouting, "You can't do that to Matt!"

She was flushed and crying. José was in shock. What was happening? He grabbed her wrists and tried to get her to relax. She was shaking her head from side to side. Her eyes appeared frenzied and her voice was harsh. José finally felt the tension in her arms relax. "Hold it, calm down. What in the world brought on that bizarre reaction?"

It took a few minutes for Anne to compose herself before she told him her life's story. She recounted being orphaned at a young age and moving from foster home to foster home, briefly detailing the horrors she experienced there.

Anne continued her story, telling José how Maria became one of her favourite patients.

"I saw Maria's ability to love unconditionally. I knew that she respected me as a competent professional, but she also recognized that I had a vulnerability hidden behind a reserved exterior meant to protect me from emotional hurt. I also suspected that she was match-making between you and me. I purposely timed my care of Maria to be there when you and Matt came to visit. I felt the love between all of you and wanted to share it, even from the outside. When Maria was released and you asked if I was available for home care, I was elated. I readily agreed as much for the extra income as an opportunity to keep in touch with you."

Once they had both finished their stories, they were surprised to realize that they were hugging each other. They looked at each other and simultaneously felt a surge of love that left them both speechless.

"Oh no, look at the time! I was to relieve Shelley twenty minutes ago so that she could get to her class. Will you come home with me? I'm sure Matt would love to see you," asked José.

Once they got to the house, Shelley was not happy as she would be late for class.

"Oh Shelley, I am so sorry. I know how important it is for you to graduate. I can't apologize enough."

"Fine," she said, "just get out of the way so I can hurry."

Matt showed up at the door, upset that Shelley was taking Chad with her. But he quickly changed his mood when he saw Anne.

José looked around at the pile of laundry and the mess in the kitchen. The condition of the place would surely have upset Maria. He started to clean up when he heard Matt ask Anne for something to eat. He wondered how he could possibly get everything done. It had been an overwhelming day.

"Anne, if you don't mind could you please make dinner for us while I tackle the mess here?"

When she didn't reply, he turned around to see why. She had a look of distress on her face. "Oh Anne, what's wrong? Are you okay?"

"I can't cook," she blurted out.

José was stumped. He had no idea how to respond.

"When I was in care, I was on clean up duty, never kitchen duty. Once I lived at Mama Murphy's, I either ate at the college cafeteria or at the restaurant where I worked. Other times, I would buy a sandwich or soup at the deli in the grocery store. I always had power bars in my backpack for snacks."

José had to try hard not to laugh. "Well, we are very lucky. Mom insisted I learn to cook as soon as I could reach the stove safely. We will not go hungry. You can do the laundry and play with Matt."

As the months went by, José and Anne spent more and more time together. They knew instinctively that they would end up together and actually began talking as if it were already decided. They planned a future together that included Matt.

José decided to sell the house rather than renovate it. The place sold quickly. He was given a generous two months to move out. He then made an appointment with Miguel Gonzales to sign the papers for the sale of the house and confirm the status of Matt.

"Well, José, you are down as the legal father. The letter she wrote giving up her custodial rights may possibly be invalid, so we will have to make an effort to locate her. Shelley is still in town but claims to this day that she has no idea where Erin and her boyfriend are, and I for one believe she is telling the truth."

José agreed and added that Shelley was moving out and Anne, his new girlfriend, would be moving in at the end of the month for a short time before he had to relinquish the house. At that point, Miguel suggested that if José and Anne were going to be partners, they should come in to write wills and sign Power of Attorney papers to protect their situation. It seemed a bit extreme, but remembering Maria's and Anne's parents' sudden deaths, José agreed that they should be covered.

He and Anne continued to do things together. Since she always used public transit, Anne had never had a driver's licence. José began giving her lessons.

\*\*\*

Anne had only lived alone for a short time but was more than eager to give up her privacy and space to move in with José and Matt. She gave notice to her landlord and arranged for the second-hand store to take back the few items she had purchased. As she was packing, she found a large envelope that she had forgotten about. It was the package she had been given by her case worker when she aged-out of care five years ago.

She took a deep breath and carefully emptied the contents onto the table. As she went through the items, she felt herself growing very angry. That's the funny thing about emotions. Her feelings had been buried for years, but once she let herself love, the gamut of emotions flowed.

The envelope contained her history. There was a newspaper clipping about the plane crash that killed her parents. The second article reported on a settlement from the airlines granting all the victims a cheque of $250,000 each towards their estates.

Anne was stunned. Where was that money that should have been her legacy? Is that why her Aunt Terry had sold their little house, moved to the city, and paid for the education of their children?

Next was a copy of her parents' last will and testament, dated from before Anne was born. It gave everything to Aunt Terry. Therefore, all assets—the plane crash settlement, a small savings account, the mortgaged house, and a small life insurance policy—went directly to Terry.

According to the documents, the Blacks had sold her parents' house and cars, paid off the credit cards, funerals, and legal expenses, and kept the remaining money. Anne could hardly contain the rage that was building inside of her. Nearly $400,000 that should have morally and ethically been for her expenses had been used for the Black family. By her estimate, they had handed her over to social services as soon as the money was safely in their bank account.

Anne was drained. She had long ago lost track of her relatives so had no idea what to do next. Did she have any legal recourse? Why hadn't the government stepped in to protect what should have been her assets?

Intense anger was another new emotion for her. She took a deep breath and opened the next envelope. It contained her parents' Canadian citizenship papers and her own papers. Outrage once again overcame her. Not only had they stolen her inheritance, but also her birth name. According to her B.C. birth certificate, her registered legal name was Julia Anna Novakova, not Anne Novak. The school report cards and other items in the envelope showed that her name was changed when she moved in with the Blacks. They had changed their own name from Cerny to disguise their ethnic background so took the liberty of Anglicizing her name as well. Just as Anne thought she would explode, someone knocked at her door. She never had guests and only José knew where she lived so she seriously considered not answering, especially since she knew her face showed signs of the tears she had been shedding. The knocking persisted and a voice called, "Delivery for Anne Novak."

Now what, more bad news? She slowly opened the door as far as the chain would reach. The man at the door was a courier for a law firm and had a registered letter for her. She had to show photo ID and sign for the envelope before he released it. Knowing he would just come back later, she produced her ID and signed.

The morning's emotions had taken a toll on her, so she decided to take a break. Eventually, her racing heart quieted. She decided to leave the big package and explore the new mysterious envelope from a lawyer.

As if she had not been through enough so far this day, fate had one more curveball to throw at her. In the large envelope were two items, a legal sized envelope and a card sized envelope. She opted to open the card first and was soon in tears again. Twenty years of not allowing herself to cry and now this day was a real flood.

It was a friendship card from her former land-lady, Mama Murphy. There was a handwritten letter enclosed.

*Dear Anne,*

*I started life as you did, with no family or support group. I took the only job I could get. I became the housekeeper and cook for an elderly, cranky man named Charles Andover. It was not an easy job, but it gave me room and board and a few dollars. Like you, my job required long hours and a uniform, so I did not have time or money for fun or shopping. After four years, Mr. Andover died, and I thought I would be alone again. But I was shocked to learn that he had willed the house to me. It seems that he also had no family. I started a boarding house to fill the rooms but soon realized that I hated cooking and cleaning. That is why I turned it into a rooming house.*

*For a time, I shared the place with Lisa Chow, your school counselor. But our love threatened her career, so she moved out. We continued to travel together during her holiday times.*

*I ran the rooming house for thirty years. As you can imagine, hundreds of young ladies have passed through the doors. Not only did you stay the longest, but you were the only one who never complained even when you rightfully could. I admired how focused you were in doing whatever it took to reach your goals. You were also the only person who took time to have a cup of tea and a visit with me.*

*If you can remember, I sold the house to a developer that had been after it for a long time. I took the money and moved into the fanciest and most expensive retirement home I could find. It costs me a lot every month, but I am enjoying the few months I have left before the cancer takes me. It's my time to be pampered; I get my hair styled every week, I get regular manicures, pedicures, and massages, and I eat like royalty.*

*As you may recall, I have no family. You are the closest I have ever had to a sister, friend, or daughter. I hope you find a man to love and be happy with. In the meantime, please accept my assets as your dowry.*

*Love Catherine Elizabeth Murphy*
*aka Mama Murphy*

Anne was numb. She slowly opened the letter from the lawyer that included a copy of Ms. Murphy's last will and testament. It was her second such document in a short time.

It stated that as soon as all attempts to find relatives were exhausted, she would inherit Catherine's entire estate that consisted of a bank account and a few pieces of jewelry. She was to go to the lawyer's office with proof of identity to receive the money and items.

What was happening to her life? All of a sudden, she had a new family history and people to love. Now it looked like she may have some money as well. Years of sacrifice and going without may soon be over.

She didn't know what to do next. Then she realized that for the first time ever, she had someone to talk to before making a decision.

As soon as José was off work, she would share her news so he could help her decide what to do. While she waited, she continued going through the items in the package that had sat unopened for over five years. What other surprises could it contain?

She sorted through various items: a certificate for finishing kindergarten, her grade one report card, her Christening papers, and a family photo from her last Christmas with her parents. More tears followed as she realized she had forgotten what her parents looked like. She studied their faces to find traces of her own appearance. A small family album brought more sadness as she thumbed through the pages of family love.

The final item was again what appeared to be a greeting card envelope. It was from her final foster parents, the Raeburns. She briefly wondered why it was in the big package and had not been handed to her when the social worker came to fill in the end-of-care documents. Anne took a breath and opened it.

It was a good luck card with a short note.

*Dear Anne,*

*It has been a pleasure to have you be a part of our extended family for three years. You were such a pleasant, hardworking, focused child. The contribution you made towards the younger children at the house will have lasting effects. I know you will be a success in life and a credit to your dear parents. Please stay in touch and let us know how you make out at Mama Murphy's and at the college.*

*Best wishes, Bev and Kevin Raeburn*

Enclosed was a cheque for $100.00. Anne cried some more. How she wished she had stayed in touch with the people closest to her since her parents. They must have wondered why she never cashed the cheque. She had often wondered why they didn't keep in touch since they knew where she was living. Maybe they thought she did not want to stay connected.

Everything was just too much. She eventually fell into an exhausted sleep.

Anne woke up feeling confused. She slowly began to recall her day of discoveries and the gamut of emotions that had overwhelmed her: Learning that her aunt, her only blood relative, had kept all the money from her parents' estate and sent her off to foster care with an Anglicized name; learning that the Raeburns had long ago cared enough to wish her well; and, the biggest shock, learning she had inherited all of Mama Murphy's estate. Anne realized she had never known Mama Murphy's real name or story. Boy, they did have a lot in common.

She decided to put off contacting the lawyer until she and José discussed the timeline of their future together. Both she and José planned to take advantage of their accumulated vacation days and go on a road trip.

*\*\**

Anne awoke the next morning still feeling drained as a result of all that she had learned. She called José to see if she could come over to his place.

"Sure, come on over. I'm taking Matt to daycare, then I'll have an hour before going to work."

When Anne arrived, José was shocked at her appearance. She poured out what she had just learned. They discussed what an impact it had on her. José agreed that she needed to see the lawyer as soon as possible. She phoned right away and was able to make an appointment with Brent Summers.

Anne took the only ID she had to the appointment, her B.C. Care Card and her Union Card. But it was more than enough because Brent had a photo of her from Mama's file.

Brent felt there was little chance of a relative emerging but could not pass over the money or jewelry until due diligence had been fulfilled.

Anne then told him about discovering that the name she had been using was not her legal name and asked if the money could be assigned in her legal name. She wanted her identity back. Brent could see no reason not to grant her request.

First Brent wanted Anne to know Catherine's story. His first job as a lawyer, many years ago, was to tell Catherine she had inherited the house from Mr. Andover. Over the years, he continued to take care of all her legal matters. When she finally decided to sell the rooming house, he handled the transaction, making sure the developer did not take advantage of her. Catherine knew she had cancer and wondered what to do with her windfall of money from the sale. He suggested that she leave it to cancer research or her friend Lisa Chow. But Catherine didn't want to give her money to charity, and she and Lisa had had a falling out a few years prior.

Brent continued. "Then she told me all about you. She wanted to reward you like Mr. Andover did with her. She had followed your career and remembered where you moved to. So finding you was easy. Proving who you are will be easy. Now about the estate. The house was in need of renovations but the property was very valuable. Once all the expenses have been paid for her burial, the remaining rent on her room at the centre taken care of, and a few medical bills paid; there will still be a very nice sum left. If the ads looking for her relatives produce no one, the money and jewelry will be yours. Do you want to know how much we may be talking about?" he finished.

"No, I have taken two weeks off work and need that time to think and plan without relying on something that might not be mine," Anne responded. She was not accustomed to good luck.

That night, Anna prepared a meal using her newly acquired skills in the kitchen. Maria's much used recipe book was still open to José's favourite meal.

Anne was surprised to discover that she enjoyed everything about cooking. The new vocabulary—sauté, fold in, mince, braise, julienne—intrigued her and the aromas that filled the kitchen delighted her. The challenge of timing so that all components were simultaneously ready was sometimes daunting. But most of all, the look on José's face as she served something simple or complicated filled her with joy.

She turned to smile when she heard José enter the room. He acknowledged her but did not come up to give her a hug or examine what she was cooking as he usually did. He seemed very nervous. Her first thought was, *Oh no, not another drama. How much are we meant to endure?* Being new to a relationship, she wondered if she should ask him if something was wrong or wait for him to offer a reason. Maybe he had a bad day at work. He did give Matt a hug.

She had a moment of panic. Maybe he was no longer interested in her. She took a deep breath and plastered a smile on her face to announce, "Okay guys, the pasta is al dente, come and get it!"

José looked at her beaming face and the delicious looking meal, bent down on his knee, and took something from his pocket.

"Anne, or Julia, or sweetheart, or dear, will you do me the honour of becoming my wife?"

Anne was so shocked. Here she was thinking he might be trying to cool the relationship, not solidify it. Her heart was beating out of control. Not knowing what else to do, she started to well up with tears as she stared at José, who looked up at her with eyes full of love.

Speechless, Anna sobbed. José asked her again as he could not quite read the message on her face.

"Please will you be my partner for life?"

She joined him on the floor and together they collapsed, laughing and crying and hugging. Matt, thinking it looked like fun, jumped on top of them and joined in the merriment.

José realized that Anne had not really answered him. "Will you please accept my mother's ring as a token of family and to formalize our engagement?"

"Yes, yes, yes," she cried. "I have never been so happy or so honoured. I can hardly believe that this is happening."

The happy couple began planning the next stage of their lives. First, they would get married. Since neither Anne nor José had ever dreamed of having an elaborate wedding, they were happy to be married in a simple ceremony with Curtis Middlemass and Miguel Gonzales acting as witnesses. Soon, Anne would have papers identifying her as Julia Anna Lopez. What a lot of name changes in such a short time.

They began planning a trip. Maria's old, reliable, small car would be replaced with a newer Minivan. They would send all the furniture to Curtis's store, deposit their important papers in the bank safety deposit box, and take a two-week road trip. When they returned, they would pick up the money for the house from José's lawyer and the inheritance from Anne's lawyer. Hopefully by then, all her papers would be in her legal name. They would also know by that time if they were done worrying about Erin Oates reappearing or people claiming to be related to Mama Murphy.

Anne finally had a family, and soon all her papers would show that she was Julia Anna Lopez.

# CHAPTER FIVE

# SPRING 1995

Debra Hartford was in a marvelous mood! She had accomplished her goal of financial independence. She had even purchased a comfortable home for her mother.

Now she was driving a fancy new motor home. The RV was a bargain thanks to her clients, the salesman and the banker. No wimpy sedan for her. With this vehicle, she could take her career to new levels, especially considering the phone call she received late last night. Debra did manage to graduate from high school thanks to an encounter with the school science teacher. Over the next years, she had amassed a very impressive black book of names and a video library of the many men and women in the town who were clients at her massage and escort business. Her list included professionals in all categories. It was handy having financial advisors, law enforcement workers, medical personnel, and retailers on her list.

Debra was on her way to reconnect with one of her first lovers, Phil Albright, who had resurfaced after five years. He had lost his job as a teacher due to sexual misconduct and had begun a new career in sex videos. He was offering her a chance to change careers.

*Damn*, she thought. She realized that because of her daydreaming she was in the wrong lane and would have to merge to the right or miss the turn-off ramp she needed to meet Phil.

\*\*\*

Jose and Anne's plan was to drive to Kamloops, then onto Prince George and return by way of Jasper. Once home, they would see the lawyers to secure their money, buy a family home, and begin life. But most important to Anne was that she would finally be able to use her legal name. All of her provincial documents were still in the name Anne Novak so she will use that for the trip. But José was already calling her Julia and Matt was actually calling her Mom. Life was so good.

So off they went!

Anne's face hurt. She could not stop smiling and laughing as they drove down the highway. She kept staring at her husband and their step-son. For the first time in two decades, she had people to love who loved her back. She had long ago given up any hope of being so happy. Life was finally great—her luck had changed.

She turned to José to say how happy she was to have found love. Instead, she let out a horrific scream as she saw a huge vehicle about to collide with them.

\*\*\*

Anne knew something was very wrong. She was waking up to unfamiliar sounds, smells, and feelings. She tried to reach for José but found movement was painful. The noises around her were strange.

She heard doctors being paged and people talking in whispers. Had she fallen asleep watching a medical show?

Anne slowly became aware that the sounds meant she was a patient in a hospital. But why?

She opened her eyes and all sorts of action began. Personnel were all over her, adjusting IVs, checking her pulse and temperature, and adjusting bandages, but not answering any of her questions.

Finally, Doctor McGraw came to talk to her.

"You have been in a terrible car accident. I am so sorry to tell you that José Lopez died on impact. The boy Matt is in Intensive Care with life threatening injuries and is not expected to recover. You have severe soft tissue damage, but thanks to the airbags, your injuries are painful but not serious. Unfortunately, you have miscarried."

Anne was numb. Slowly, she realized that someone with a very serious demeanor was talking to her.

"Pardon," she muttered. "I didn't understand what you said."

Dr. McGraw didn't know whether telling her all the bad news at once was overwhelming, but there didn't seem to be much choice. She rephrased what she had said.

"Anne, as a result of a car accident, your husband José Lopez is dead."

"No, that's not true. We just got married. We're starting our life together."

"I am very sorry Anne, but it is true. Matt Lopez is in serious condition and will probably not recover."

"No, that's not true. He's just a boy. He already lost his mother now you say his father is dead. What kind of nightmare is this? We're on our honeymoon, going on our first ever vacation. We formed a family. How can any of this be true? We were happy. How dare you say such things! Wake me from this nightmare!"

When Anne stopped screaming, Dr. McGraw repeated. "Your injuries are not serious thanks to the airbags. However, unfortunately, you have miscarried."

"I was pregnant? I would have had my own baby to love?"

Anne tried to get out of bed. "I need to see José. I need to see Matt. I don't believe you."

She ranted and cried so hard that she was sedated.

Hours later, she awoke to the soothing presence of a nurse. Her name was Mandy, and she was full of empathy, and calmness. When Anne felt ready, Mandy called for the counselor.

The counselor offered her deepest sympathies. Then she began discussing the legal and logistical matters.

"What is the relationship between you, José, and Matt?" was her first question.

Between sobs, Anne explained that José was her husband and Matt was his son.

"Okay, do you have any legal custodial rights to Matt? Decisions have to be made about his future."

Anne said that Matthew's mother had given full custodial rights to José. The paper proving that fact was in the possession of lawyer Miguel Gonzales, in Rangeland. When the counselor left, Nurse Mandy came back to comfort Anne. With a little help, Anne was soon asleep again.

The next morning, when Anne was sitting in a wheelchair, another person was there to see her.

He was a well-dressed, professional-looking man who she thought might be another doctor. "Hello, Anne. My name is Walter Brown. I am so sorry to hear about the accident that befell your lovely young family. Please accept my condolences. I am a lawyer here to help you settle the account of the accident."

Anne frowned. "The account of the accident? Is that how you describe what happened? I lost my husband and son and a baby. It wasn't an accident, it was a tragedy."

Walter did not respond but did change his demeanor from sympathetic to more formal.

"This is a report from ICBC detailing the accident and offering you three weeks of therapy, plus two weeks in a motel. There will also be a cheque for the book value of the vehicle. Also, here is a generous cheque for the wrongful death of José and the medical expenses for Matt." His smooth-talking explanation was that she could get more money perhaps if she went to civil court but it would take years of litigation.

"I understand that you are distraught now and I sympathize with your situation. However, the hard facts are that the legal issues need to be settled. If I could get you to sign these papers regarding a settlement it will be one less thing for you to be concerned about. Then you can focus on getting better."

Anne was confused. Was she obligated to deal with this now? She had learned through José's story not to sign something without reading it. Her instinct told her not to trust this man, but her need to take care of everything made her feel obliged to sign.

She accepted the pen and was about to write her name on the indicated line when Nurse Mandy came in to check on Anne. She was shocked to see her talking to Walter Brown. Anne looked ready to sign some papers. Mandy knew that Mr. Brown was Debra Hartford's lawyer and should not be talking to Anne.

Mandy quickly interrupted, removed the pen from Anne's hand, and said, "Come along, we're late for therapy. Paperwork will have to wait."

With that, she got behind the wheelchair and quickly ushered Anne out of the room. Walter was calling after her, but she continued down the hall and into a room for employees only.

Once away from the lawyer, Mandy explained that Walter was the lawyer for the driver of the RV that hit them and should not be taking advantage of Anne in her current state. Not only that, but it was a blatant conflict of interest. Mandy suggested Anne contact Harry Nichols, who was known to be an honest lawyer. She even offered to phone him and asked him to come to the hospital to meet Anne and advise her on all the issues she needed to deal with.

As promised, Mandy phoned Harry's office. Her call was sent to an answering machine. After the usual recording, the message went on to say, "If the call is an emergency, please call my cell phone." The number followed. She decided it was an emergency, so called the number.

***

For over twenty years, the Nichols and the Carsons had owned neighbouring cabins at the head of Deer Lake. Many fond memories were attached to the location. However, since all the children had left home, they no longer used the retreat over the winter months. Therefore, every spring it was necessary to go up the lake and get the cabins ready for use over the summer and into the fall.

The women aired out the cabins, freshened the linen, stocked the pantry, and cleaned whatever was necessary. The men got the water system and generators working, moored the boats, raked the beach, and stacked the wood for the fire pit and wood stove.

Work detail was over so the four of them were enjoying a drink by the crackling fire. The evening conversation was full of reminiscing about all the wonderful times the two families had shared at the lake.

"Wow," sighed Coralee Carson, "I had forgotten how much work the first day up here was. I'm ready to curl up with my book until I fall asleep. Good night, all."

"Hang on," called Lesley Nichols, "I'm with you. I'm ready to curl up with my knitting. One more grandchild is on the way!"

As the women disappeared into their respective cabins, Frank Carson turned to his longtime friend Harry Nichols and said, "I was wondering when they would hit the sack. Now we can have another night cap and talk about real important issues. What time are we going fishing tomorrow?"

"I bought a new rod and reel that Lesley doesn't know about yet so I need to catch an impressive fish to prove that it was a worthwhile investment." Harry chuckled.

Frank, the town's chief detective, and Harry, one of the town's top lawyers, stayed up an hour later than their wives discussing the events of town life. On rare occasions, Harry would be defence counsil for some of the people Frank had arrested. But normally, he was very content with the everyday legal affairs of real estate, wills and civic matters, and traffic issues. The two men turned to discussing how their wives, now that they had retired from teaching, were hinting that the men should also retire.

Soon, the men put out the campfire, brought the glasses and dishes inside, and retired to their respective cabins.

\*\*\*

Harry was surprised when he heard his phone ring. Who could that be? Darn cell phones, meant to be a convenience but sometimes were an interruption.

"Hello Mandy, if you are calling my cell, it must certainly be an emergency. Tell me what is happening."

"Oh, Harry, Walter Brown who is representing Debra in that horrible fatal car crash was trying to get Anne, the survivor to sign some papers. I was able to stop her but she is so vulnerable I fear he may return." Harry was shocked by the news.

"Good job Mandy. I'm at the lake now but will be down in two days. Thanks for stopping Walter from intimidating Anne.

Please keep her safe." He promised to see Anne when he returned.

Two days later, Harry went to see Anne. His first impression of her was that she was a bewildered, sad woman who looked so small and pale in the hospital bed. Mandy introduced Harry to Anne and assured her he was trustworthy. He explained to her that there were a lot of legal issues that needed to be sorted out.

First and foremost, her legal right to make decisions regarding José's funeral arrangements and Matt's medical care had to be established. Anne was able to tell Harry that she and José had just written wills and signed Power of Attorney documents before leaving for their road trip. The items were at the office of lawyer Miguel Gonzales in Rangeland. Harry then asked about burial preferences for José and what assets he had in his own and joint names.

Harry phoned Mr. Gonzales at once. When he was connected he stated, "Hello, Mr. Gonzales, My name is Harold Nichols, I am a lawyer in Deer Lake. I am representing one of your clients, Anne Lopez in the matter of the horrific accident that killed Jose and has left the boy Matthew on life support. I need to know what the legal status of Anne as she may need to make some important decisions about the future of the boy and the internment of José."

"Thank you for calling." responded Mr. Gonzales, "In Rangeland we only heard about the accident through the local news channel. I have been trying to find out who I should contact. I can assure you that before they left for their holiday, José and Anne were legally married, and had all assets put in both names, including the care of Matthew. I can fax you copies right away. José was a very well respected member of the community. I will do everything to assist you. Thanks for caring for Anne. Please keep in touch."

Once he had that information, he passed it on to the hospital board members. Matt was still on life support and the hospital was under pressure to pre-serve his vital organs for transplant but needed Anne's authority to take the next steps.

Anne was reluctant at first but accepted the fact that Matt was brain dead. When she went to sign the papers, she hesitated, pointed to his name, and then changed her mind about the error. The name on the form read Matthew Lopez, not Matthew Oates as per his birth certificate. She did not point out the error as she realized that José was the only constant in Matt's life and had a right to his name. She was led to the ICU to say goodbye to Matt.

Anne could not believe her eyes as she looked at her beautiful son, full of cuts and bruises and all sorts of medical tubes. She held his hands and told him how much she and José loved him. She didn't know how she could carry on. Finally, emotionally spent, she kissed him good bye and tried to stand up.

Mandy ushered her back to her room and sat with her until she fell into a deep sleep courtesy of an injection. Harry left to do more follow up on funeral and accident issues.

The next day, Harry arrived at Anne's hospital room with a list of things to be done regarding José's and Matt's remains. Since Anne was without a doubt the administrator of the estate, she and Harry could easily dispense with a lot of legalities. Acting as her lawyer, he had already obtained copies of the death certificates and arranged for the cremation of both José and Matt.

Then it was an easy matter of going through the guide provided by the funeral home and checking off the necessary post-death tasks.

Harry would deal with BC Medical, ICBC, and BCAA regarding a settlement on the value of the destroyed vehicle and money for her physiotherapy treatment and temporary motel accommodation.

Next, government services would be contacted to cancel José's SIN and inquire about death benefits. It seemed an onerous task but Harry was aware of the tricks to settle an uncomplicated will. Harry was a unique lawyer who was given his nickname "Hurry Up" because he pushed all his cases through the system as quickly as possible. His reputation was that he streamlined all items through to save the court valuable time and the client time and money for fees.

Anne was so confused by it all and was ever so grateful for the advice and help of Harry and the comfort, even on her time off, from Mandy. They offered her legal help and compassion throughout the process of having José and Matt cremated. On their advice, she sent an obituary announcement to the Rangeland News. She was surprised to receive a card at the hospital from José's coworkers who had sent a donation on his behalf to the burn unit at the local hospital. It was the designated charity of the hall and José had often helped in the fundraising events.

Next Harry, in his usual manner, helped Anne face the legal quagmire of the accident itself. Debra had been held one hundred percent liable for the devastating accident. Regardless of the horror of the accident, all she was charged with was distracted driving for looking at her GPS screen. She received the minimum fine and was ordered to do one hundred hours of community service.

Anne was feeling ill. Harry had arranged a meeting to settle a civil action that he had initiated against Debra Hartford for wrongful death. The room felt claustrophobic to Anne. A mediator, Harry, Anne, Debra, and Walter Brown were seated at a round table. It was impossible to look at the killer of her loved ones or listen to the dialogue between the two lawyers and mediator. Debra, on the other hand, appeared bored with the whole procedure.

Harry began, "Walter, we all agreed that this matter should be easily be dealt with today, thus saving the plaintiff and defendant months of angst as both ladies want to leave town as quickly as possible. We are asking for compensation for the loss of two lives, pain and suffering of the victim, and reimbursement of burial costs. Also, considering your lack of judgment in approaching Anne at the hospital, we feel that $750,000.00 would be a reasonable amount to end this disturbing situation."

Walter shuffled some papers before responding. "Harry, with all due respect, as you know, these types of litigation can take years at a huge emotional and financial cost to all involved. But, since speed is of the essence, as you so rightfully pointed out, it will take time to secure that much money. However, if you are willing to accept $600,000 we can write a draft for that now."

Anne burst into tears when she realized that a price had been put on the lives of the only two people in the world that she loved.

"How can you put a price tag on the lives of the people you killed? My husband was a good honest hard working man. My son was a delightful healthy boy. My baby was just beginning life." She cried in despair.

She became conscious that everyone was looking at her. Harry gently covered her hand with his. "Anne, Mr. Brown has made an acceptable settlement. I would recommend that you and I step outside to read it. I can explain it in simple terms. Then you can decide what to do. If you accept it, then it will be the end. If you reject it may take years to settle with you dealing daily with the pain, riddled with uncertainty and expense".

"Harry, I trust you, and if you are okay with the offer, then so am I. Show me where to sign. I need to find somewhere and some way to grieve."

They reentered the room and signed all the papers.

Walter handed the bank draft to Harry, Debra hugged and kissed Walter, and they all left the room.

It had only been a few weeks since the court case, but Debra had already paid the fine and completed her hours of community service, often logging two hours for every hour worked thanks to her clients.

\*\*\*

Anne continued to allow herself to be called Anne. Somehow the name Julia was sacred to her and José, and she wanted to keep it that way for now. Harry helped her leave the hospital and get a motel room in the area so she would be able to continue her therapy.

Anne had one more request for Harry. Would he please drive her to Rangeland? He immediately agreed as he was curious to meet Miguel, the lawyer with whom he had been corresponding since the accident.

Before leaving for Rangeland, Anne asked to go to the funeral home. Harry drove there, dropped Anne off, and went to fill his car with gas.

When Anne entered the building, she was greeted by a receptionist who, when told why Anne was there, went to the back room and emerged carrying two bags. "I need to prepare you. The bags are heavy. I have alerted our business in Rangeland to expect you. They will help you with the details of the burials. We are the office are so sorry for your losses and wish you well in the future."

Anne went outside and saw that Harry waiting for her.

The drive to Rangeland was done in near silence as both Anne and Harry were busy with their thoughts. When they arrived in Rangeland, Harry drove to the funeral home.

"I will wait here for you then drive you to Mr. Gonzales office."

"That won't be necessary," she replied. "I can handle it. Plus I have other places I need to go to, so I'll meet you at the Tim Hortons in two hours, okay?" Anne said.

Harry sensed she needed to be alone, so quickly agreed, although he was very curious what she would be doing for the next two hours. He felt it would be better if he accompanied her to see the lawyer, but she obviously felt confident in dealing with the issues on her own.

Once inside the funeral home, Anne was escorted into office of a clerk.

"Hello, Anne. I was so sad to hear about the horrendous accident. The Deer Lake office called to say that you would be in today."

Anne worked hard to stay composed as she spoke in a low voice. "I would like the urns to be buried with José's mother Maria, and the plaques with their names secured at the site."

"Yes, we can certainly do that for you. I will need to coordinate with the cemetery staff for a time. It may take up to a week."

"That's fine. I will pay for everything now, plus extra for the site to be maintained." Anne reached for her purse and paid with what was supposed to be their holiday money.

Once she paid the invoice, she turned to and said, "Could you call a taxi to take me to the cemetery?"

"No need, I will get our driver to take you there."

Once at the cemetery, Anne was pleased to see that Maria's grave had been kept tidy

As she knelt by the grave, she thought about how her life had changed because of Maria.

She offered a short prayer. "Dear Maria, thank you for taking me into your home and life. I brought my bad luck with me and now three people are dead. I hope someday I can atone for the devastation I have brought you. I loved you as a mother figure and a friend. Goodbye, dear lady."

Once she was done, Anne walked back into town to quiet her thoughts. It took her fifteen minutes to arrive at the law office.

Once inside, Anne went directly to Miguel's office. The friendly receptionist greeted her with a big hug and expressed her horror at the loss of José and Matt.

Miguel walked towards her and embraced her. "Oh, Anne, we are all so devastated by the horrible accident and your enormous loses. It is an absolute nightmare. Please come in and sit down. I knew and respected the Lopez family for years. Maria worked so hard, as did José. They both loved you like you were family."

"Miguel, I'm still in a state of denial. I'm so fortunate that you had José and me write up the will and other documents. It made the nightmare a little easier to deal with. Now I find myself alone again, but it is worse after having learned to love. I even lost our baby, who could have been someone to love forever. But now let's get to what happens next."

Miguel said, "Because of the work we did before, the will was easy to take care of so did not require probate. Your name was already added to all of José's bank accounts, and the RRSPs he inherited from his mother had you as the beneficiary. There were no other assets." He handed her a file containing all of the documents.

"Thank you for all you have done. I have no idea what to do next." Anne lamented. "I guess it's a blessing I don't have to worry about getting a job yet."

Anne left with copies of the death certificates, the cheques from Walter Brown on behalf of Debra Hartford, and the ICBC money.

Next, she went to the office of her lawyer, Brent Summers, to see about her inheritance from Mama

Murphy. The office was only a block away so she walked, switching her mind from José's estate to that of Mama Murphy. Despite the fact that she did not have an appointment, she walked into the office. She was just wondering where the receptionist was when Brent emerged from his office. He greeted her with hugs and condolences. Once seated in the office, Brent began to update her on the issues he was dealing with on her behalf.

Because business in the office had been slow, he was able to concentrate fully on her file. There would be no trouble in starting an account in her legal name, closing her other accounts, and re-depositing the money in a new account. He had already spoken to the bank manager who was ready for her to visit.

Next came even more good news. No one had surfaced claiming to be related to Catherine Elizabeth Murphy aka Mama Murphy. The total estate, including the sale of the boarding house and minus outstanding expenses, is $956,720.62!"

It took a long time for Anne to regain her composure. She was stunned.

What kind of horrid karma was coming to mock her?

With the cheques from Deer Lake in her pocket plus Mama's estate, she was worth nearly two million dollars. The shock was compounded when she realized that she had absolutely no one to share it with.

Once again she was sobbing uncontrollably. Brent left her to grieve. When she recovered, they went back to business.

Anne then asked Brent if he could keep all her money in trust. Once she was finished with her rehab, she would be better able to make a decision about her future. Then she could open all accounts in the name of Julia Anna Novakova. He was baffled, but agreed to hold onto her money in trust until she was ready to move on. Before she left, he gave her a jewelry chest that had been willed to her by Mama.

With a heavy heart and swollen face, Anne went to the park where she and José had spent so many happy hours playing with Matt.

Eventually, she walked to the bank armed with copies of the death certificate and will. Since the teller was expecting her, the process went smoothly. She withdrew three thousand dollars in cash from the account and signed up for a credit card. Then she left to meet Harry.

Harry was becoming concerned as it was thirty minutes past the time they were to meet. Finally, he spotted her walking towards him, clutching what appeared to be a wooden box.

Since it was obvious she had been crying, he did not question her. They drove back to Deer Lake in silence. When they reached the motel he invited her to his home for a meal. She declined his invitation, thanked him for his concern, and assured him all went well in Rangeland. Harry reminded her that he would be available any time she needed him.

Once inside, Anne lay on the bed and cried. What was she to do now? Life was so much easier when she had no one to love or to love her. It was emptier than it had ever been before. Now she had a lot of money but nothing else.

She was interrupted by a phone call.

***

It was only Thursday, but Detective Frank Carson was already looking forward to the weekend at the cabin. Just one last item to take care of then he could get ready to leave the office. He let out a deep sigh, made a notation on paper, closed a file, and stamped it Case Closed. He was not at all at peace with the case. It was a car accident with two fatalities, a father and his four-year-old son. The wife was trying to deal with her loss, plus all the paperwork necessary.

The final detail of the case was all that was left to do. And, without a doubt, it was the most difficult.

Frank reached for the phone and asked his receptionist to connect him with Anne Lopez at the Deer Lake Motel. When the connection was made, the call was transferred to him. "Hello," he said to the motel clerk. "This is Detective Carson; please connect me with Anne Lopez's room."

"I'll connect you sir. I just saw her return to her room, so I know she's in."

The phone rang four times before Anne answered it. "Hello," she said in a toneless voice.

"Mrs. Lopez, this is Detective Carson. I'm finalizing the paperwork regarding the tragic accident that claimed the lives of your family. Unfortunately, I must tell you that there is one more unpleasant task you must do as the next of kin. The destroyed car is being released from the police compound and it will be necessary for you to sign the forms and arrange for it to be towed to a salvage yard."

There was silence on the other end of the line. "Mrs. Lopez, do you understand what needs to be done?"

"Yes, sir. I will see to it." She hung up the phone.

Frank slowly replaced the receiver as well. In all his years, he had not dealt with such a sad case. It hurt him deeply to know she was so alone and devastated.

\*\*\*

Anne was numb. How could she even think about the vehicle that was to be the start of a new beginning but ended up being a cruel ending?

Later, Mandy phoned to check up on Anne.

"Hi Anne, How was the trip to Rangeland?"

"Hi Mandy, Everything legal is done. I should feel some closure but Detective Carson just phoned."

"What did he want? Are there still more issues to deal with?" asked Mandy.

"I need to go to the Police Compound and have the car removed. I don't know how I can possibly face it."

Mandy immediately told her about Apex Auto Wreckers and Scrap Yard and assured her that Brad would take care of everything for her. She had twenty-four hours to act.

"Oh Mandy, you have been an angel."

It was the straw that broke the camel's back. She was overwhelmed with emotions. Anger, fury, hatred welled up in her and she exploded. Why was she alone once again?

She sat on the bed and punched the pillows as she raged:

why her loving parents were taken from her at a young age;

why her relatives took her inheritance and family identity; why the government system left her with no support;

why only one foster family and a landlady appeared to care about her;

why she spent years burying all emotions only to have them reborn then taken away again;

why the accident caused her to miscarry a baby she had no idea had been conceived;

why the justice system had let José and Matt's killer get away with a fine;

why that horrid lawyer had tried to get her to sign off on the accident; and

why she had to experience the horrific, inconsolable loss of José and Matt.

And now they want her to see the death car?

It was all too much. Ice cold blood ran through her veins. She needed some kind of revenge. She needed to get even with life.

She cleaned herself up and decided on a long therapeutic walk to the outskirts of town to find the scrap yard. She hoped the sheer physical activity would bring her calm. She would deal with the car in the morning after her last physiotherapy appointment.

# CHAPTER SIX

# SPRING 1995

It sure was hard to believe that five years had gone by so quickly. Brad had taken over complete management of the business, hired his sister to do the office work, and had already taken on an apprentice, Mark Hunter, to help out. The happiest part of his life was going home and playing outside with Bobby. The boy was a natural athlete and loved playing with his dad. Monika studied a few hours a week, leaving Bobby at the college daycare, but she thrived on being a mom. She had been working with her parents for five years and was being groomed to take over the business as she was on the verge of qualifying as a chartered accountant. Her sister Mavis had gone to university and was also about to graduate as a chartered accountant. The two sisters would soon be running the firm as their parents planned to retire.

Bobby was doted on by both sets of grandparents and both aunts. Every family event was celebrated with gusto. Since Bobby's grandparents and his two aunts were all best friends, every occasion—Easter, Labour Day, Thanksgiving, Christmas, birthdays, anniversaries—was an excuse to get together at the lake or at the family homes.

Monika and Brad had decided to expand their family and have another child. But despite trying almost daily to conceive, there was no pregnancy. They decided to go to the doctor for a full physical to see if there was a problem or if they were just trying too hard.

Monika had a clean bill of health—all systems were healthy.

At nine o'clock on Friday, Brad was on his way to the clinic to see the results of his fertility tests.

An hour later, Brad felt dead. No, if he were dead he would not have any feelings. He wanted his brain to stop. His heart had exploded. He could not breathe. He wanted to be dead. How could his perfect life come tumbling down with two little sentences?

His test results were in with the awful news that his sperm count was so low that he was nearly sterile. "There are a few reasons for this condition: low testosterone, thyroid issues, or excessive exercise, especially during puberty," explained Doctor Tait, their long-time family physician.

Dr. Tait continued. "Brad do you recall two weeks ago when Bobby fell and cut his leg? His femoral artery was severed and he was weak from blood loss. A quick check confirmed Monika was the same blood type so we started a transfusion. Then you arrived from work and wanted to be prepped so you could also donate blood. I drew a sample of your blood just as the nurse announced it wasn't needed as Bobby had received enough from Monika. There was no need to process the sample immediately."

Brad frowned and squirmed impatiently, wondering what the doctor was leading to. He was still reeling from being told he had a very low sperm count.

"However, when I went to file the results, I discovered that it was incompatible with Bobby's," continued Dr. Tait. "I wondered if for some reason the sample had become contaminated, so when you came in for your physical, you will recall that we took a blood sample. We checked the results, but they confirmed what the first tests showed. You cannot be Bobby's father."

"Don't be ridiculous!" shouted Brad. "You better check again. Monika and I have been together forever. She was a virgin when we first had sex, as was I."

"I checked it three times to be absolutely sure. Bobby has DNA from Monika but not you. She is definitely the mother."

That meant that nearly five years ago, Monika had been unfaithful. He had loved her since they were five. She was his whole world—a part of him. How could this be true?

When? Where? Who? His brain was on fire, his heart was racing. His life was now a nightmare, a farce, a lie. How could he have been so much in love with a dream? He needed to think. He needed a plan. He needed to think of a plan. What should he do next?

He had raced out of the clinic and into his car. Too distraught to drive, he sat behind the steering wheel shouting and crying and pounding his fists on his head and steering wheel.

He did not know how long he sat in the car before he became aware that people were beginning to stare at him. He drove to his office where he could be alone for a while. Kristie and Mark were told not to disturb him.

A wave of nausea overcame him. He vomited and heaved until he was dry. Then he sobbed until he was dry. Then a kind of quiet overcame him as he knew what he needed to do. Slowly, he walked over to the locked cabinet where unclaimed and illegal items were stored until they could be delivered to the police.

With determination and premeditation, he unlocked the box and chose what he needed.

Acting as if he was still at work, Brad loaded the pickup with some metal roads and tire rims. Then with cold determination, he drove home to where Monika was awaiting results of his fertility tests.

As usual, Bobby ran to greet him, expecting to get picked up, twirled around, and hugged. Instead, Brad pushed him aside and stared at Monika. Bewildered by his actions, she asked him what the doctor had told him. Fearing that he had a serious medical problem, she rushed over to hug him. He pushed her away and with an ice cold voice asked, "WHO IS YOUR SON'S FATHER"

Shocked by such a question, Monika just stared at him, unable to comprehend or answer such a bizarre statement. "Brad, how can you ask such a question? Bobby was conceived by the power of our love for each other. We have always been together. What are you thinking? You're very upset and you're scaring me. Sit down, I've just made some tea, let me pour you a cup and you can tell me what's wrong."

Monika went into the kitchen and with shaking hands and a confused mind, took her time making a fresh pot of tea. She could not comprehend what was causing Brad to act so strangely. She poured some tea into Brad's favourite cup—the one that said World's Best Dad.

As she returned to the living room, she saw Brad forcing Bobby to drink some of her tepid tea. As she approached, Brad grabbed Bobby roughly, placed him in his chair, and told him to quick whimpering and to stay in his chair.

"Why are you yelling at Bobby? Why are you forcing tea down his throat? Since when have you ever been rough with him? Especially when he has a sore leg—the stitches were only just removed. You're definitely extremely upset about something. Bobby, sweetheart, do as daddy says and just sit in your chair."

Monika gently put her arm around Brad. He recoiled as if he had been burned.

More confused than ever, Monika picked up her tea. Brad sat down across from her and stared at her with eyes full of hate.

"Brad, please tell me the results of your tests. You're scaring me. I've never seen you so angry. If you're ill, we can deal with it together." Once again, she reached out for him. Once again, he recoiled.

"First," he snarled, "the doctor informed me I have an extremely low sperm count. I probably always have had. But the most surprising news is the fact that DNA shows that I AM NOT BOBBY'S FATHER. So who is?" Brad stopped to catch his breath. Tears of rage stung his eyes. Monika felt the colour drain from her face. Her body went cold. She stared at him and felt herself growing faint.

Brad continued, "As we once figured, you got pregnant the night of the big game. That was our first time having sex. So what I need to know and have always wondered is, where were you during the half hour the celebration was happening? Why were you so emotional when we finally did meet? And why did you want to have sex right away after years of insisting on celibacy?" accused Brad.

Monika slowly recalled with horror what had happened after the game.

> *Upset that she thought Brad had ignored her, she had run outside behind the gym to try to make sense of what had just happened. She feared a change in their twelve-year relationship. Suddenly, she realized she was not alone. She looked up and saw Phil Albright. He was also holding back tears as he felt that Brad had stolen his last chance to be the MVP. He walked over and asked why she wasn't celebrating with Brad. Holding back sobs, she explained that Brad had not waited for her.*
>
> *Phil said, "When Brad stole the pass that was meant for me, he ruined any chance I had to finally be the MVP. There was no reason for him to once again steal*

all the kudos and limelight. I thought he was my friend and knew how much I was counting on the game to make a difference for me and my chance at a sports scholarship."

They clung to each other in shared disappointment. Phil, an experienced seducer, was soon kissing and caressing Monika. Skillfully, he lifted her mini cheerleading skirt and lowered his sport shorts. He suddenly realized that the best revenge on Brad would be the first to have sex with Monika, the proud virgin. Monika was inexperienced and slow to respond. When she realized what he was doing, she became mortified and shocked, screaming and pulling back. "What are you doing? Stop, leave me alone!"

Phil promised her that what happened was a horrible mistake and it would always be their secret. But it was too late. He had ejaculated all over her.

Monika then composed herself, monitored her breathing, and ran back into the nearly deserted changing room. She grabbed her street clothes, had a thorough shower, and left to find Brad.

Monika was stunned. No, it could not be. She felt extremely nauseous and faint. She tried to answer Brad but felt herself passing out. She tried to talk. To procrastinate, she gulped down the rest of her tea. It tasted as awful as the atmosphere in the room. Her mind was a mess. She was stunned as her memory zeroed in on the worst ten minutes of her life. She did not think that Phil had penetrated her, but he had ejaculated all over her. She tried to speak but felt herself getting lightheaded.

"I want Mommy," cried Bobby. His sobbing was not affecting Brad's calculated movements. Bobby attempted to get out of the chair but Brad held him in place. "I told you to stay in your chair," he shouted at the distraught boy.

Bobby's cries changed to whimpers, and then he appeared to fall asleep. A small sip of the tainted tea was enough to quiet him.

Meanwhile, Monika was muttering almost incoherently. Brad stared at her. Then he thought he heard her say Phil.

Enraged, he screamed, "You gave yourself to Phil. Phil! That immoral sleaze? Why? He had sex with almost every girl in the senior grades. You can't be serious."

Brad watched as Monika appeared to faint. She fell to the floor, breaking the teacup as she dropped. He started screaming and ranting into the quiet room.

"I was destined to be in the National Sports Hall of Fame, not working like a labourer in a dead-end town. I was meant to be father of the year, not married to a whore raising the bastard child of my arch enemy. First Kristie was born so I was no longer the centre of attention at home. Then Phil moves to town and encroached on my role as best all-around athlete. Now this!" He wanted to destroy the house, but felt his rage slowly dissipate and a strange calm take over.

Brad sat down, breathing deeply. As if he was in a TV crime drama, he assessed the situation. He felt for a pulse even though it repulsed him to touch Monika. He picked up the broken cup, , then went to the computer to type out a note wearing rubber gloves.

Methodically, he picked up his huge gym bag and without emotion or empathy, threw Monika's body into it. The phone would not stop ringing so he smashed it and threw it into the bag along with her purse.

Next, he grabbed her suitcase, nicely packed for their planned romantic weekend getaway. He threw everything into the back of his truck and sped off, not giving another thought to Bobby.

\*\*\*

Ruth Wilson was proud of herself—nearly seventy years old and as active, fit, and healthy as possible.

Just last week, a carload of teenagers had pulled up beside her to ask if she would like a ride. She smiled as she remembered the looks on their faces as she turned and they saw she was not as young as her size, speed, and clothes had implied.

Wearing the latest fashion had always been important to Ruth. Today she was sporting her newest outfit—a colour-coordinated jogging suit, hand band, and runners. Her water bottle, disposable camera, keys, and a snack fitted perfectly into her modern fanny pack.

Today she was on her usual power walk—a little later than usual because her gossipy neighbours had come for coffee. She wouldn't get home until after twelve at this rate

Because of the extra coffee she'd had that morning, Ruth had to quickly step off the gravel road and into the trees for a quick personal moment.

Ruth was just about to squat when she became aware of noises behind her. She quickly stood up and was immediately incensed when she spotted a man throwing garbage into a ravine. Her first thought was to yell at him but instinct warned her not to, so instead she watched in horror. As a militant environmentalist, she served on many committees and wrote numerous letters about the destruction of the fragile environment.

Ruth began taking photos with the small camera she always carried with her in case she saw something worth recording. She also had pad and paper to make note of each photo. Today she used it to quickly make a sketch of the man and his truck as he threw bags into the ravine. When he was done, he sped away.

Still fuming, Ruth started towards where the truck had been parked. Once she was sure he was gone, she walked towards what she considered to be a crime scene. Ruth had watched enough CSI TV shows to know how important it was to preserve and document the evidence. She treaded carefully around, taking photos or everything, including the items in the ravine.

Full of righteous indignation, she power walked to the drug store to bring in her film.

"Hello," she called to the attendant. "I need this film developed right now. There are only a few pictures on it but it's vital to have it ASAP."

"Well, Miss Ruth, you are always in a hurry. I will do my best. Drop in tomorrow afternoon. If for any reason I can do it today, I will call you."

Ruth continued home to compose a letter, complete with sketches to shame this incredibly bad citizen! She was so furious that she skipped having a shower so she wouldn't forget any details. Once the letter passed her editing, she made copies for the press, the mayor, and Frank Carson, head of the police department. Still full of energy, she decided to hand deliver the letters rather than rely on the post office. It was Friday after all, and the letters may not be delivered until mid-week. She wanted immediate action. She placed the letters in her small backpack and took off on her bike to get to the offices before closing time.

\*\*\*

Anne walked into an office with a plaque on the door reading Brad Andrew – Manager. She spotted a man who was in obvious distress.

The man was pacing back and forth muttering to himself. His face was flushed, and his eyes were wild. She wondered if she should leave as quietly as she had entered. In her hesitation, the man turned and looked at her with shock.

"No, this is not possible!" he yelled. "You are gone for good." Brad could not believe how much the woman at his door looked like Monika.

Kristie came running to see what was distressing him.

He stopped her at the door and said, "Everything is fine. I have a customer inside. You and Mark can take off for the rest of the day."

Kristie was surprised by his behaviour. Usually, he would introduce her to the customer. This time, she did not even see who the customer was. Oh well, she was happy to take off early as it was a beautiful day. She and Mark had just started dating and would enjoy the extra time together.

Brad's heart was racing as he tried to look at her. She was so much like Monika - her size, her colouring, even her choice of casual wear. Brad composed himself and took another look at the woman sitting there.

It was obvious she had been crying, so he gave her a minute to compose herself before he asked, "What can I do for you?"

"My name is Anne. Mandy said you could help me."

Tearfully, she explained that the police compound had told her that she must arrange to clear her belongings from her car and arrange for it to be towed to the salvage yard.

"Certainly, I can help you." Brad took out a form and began asking her relevant questions. He soon realized that she was the lone survivor from the accident caused by Debra Hartford. She confirmed that she was.

Then she broke down and told him about her life that had once been so desolate but was finally turning around. Both she and José had had very lonely childhoods full of work and study. They found each other, and with his son, they were going to form a family. But now, once again, she had nobody to share love with.

Brad was at a loss as to how to respond and found he was comforting her. Before long, he blurted out his own story that was diametrically opposed to hers.

According to his story, he had, up until today, lived a perfect life; a wonderful childhood, loving parents, success at school and sports, and he had married his childhood sweetheart and they had a wonderful son. But it all changed today. His life had become a sham.

Suddenly, an idea began to form in his devious, damaged mind. He told Anne he would take care of her car so she didn't have to see it. He asked her to come back in two hours to sign the papers and to hear his brilliant plan.

When Anne left Brad's office, she walked back to the motel for another good cry, checked out, and wandered about carrying a box and a small bag holding her few possessions. She took the journal she had purchased to record her first road trip. It was blank as they had not even finished the first day. Was it just another sad reminder?

She did not know what to do. Should she see Brad or just get on a bus and go . . . where? She decided to go back to the salvage yard as it seemed like a decision about her future may have been made for her.

Anne listened in fascinated horror as Brad outlined a way to ease both their lives.

"Today I learned that Bobby is not my son. When I confronted my wife, she cried and said she would leave but not take the boy as this is his home and there are lots of relatives around that love him. She had her suitcase packed and left in a car that pulled up. I didn't know what to do, so I gave Bobby some tea mixed with powdered sleeping pills so he could be safely left alone while I figured out what to do."

Anne was appalled at not only the idea of drugging a child, but of leaving him alone for an indefinite amount of time. "Have you any idea what may happen when he wakes up groggy? He could hurt himself, and when he realizes he's alone, he may do something dangerous." As she said this, she realized this man should not be in charge of a helpless child. So she listened to his plan.

"I lost a wife and son. You lost a husband and a son. But my boy is alive and unwanted. I think we can even out our karma. Why don't you take the boy? That way you have someone to love and I give up something that was never mine. I think it's possible."

Anne was in a state of shock. How could this be happening? Then she remembered her earlier rage and her need to get revenge from life. Her first response had been disbelief. This man was willing to give away a child as if he were a used item of no more value. She could not fathom being part of such a plot. Then her thought turned to what the child needed and what she needed. Maybe it would work.

As her shock turned into abhorrence, then back to the fury she had felt earlier, Anne found herself thinking how it could actually work out. She had Matt's birth certificate in the name of James Matthew Oates, but Matt's death certificate said Matthew Lopez. She had finalized the process of changing her name from Anne Novak to Julia Anna Novakova. Even the initials would be different. She had access to nearly two million dollars so would not need a job. Her driver's licence could prove to be an issue, as she only had an interim one, which would expire soon.

The plan was that she would take Bobby, change his name to James Mathew Oates, and disappear as Anne Novak and someday become Julia Anna Novakova. The first few days would be crucial.

Brad went to the office safe. He took out a woman's driver's licence whose information nearly resembled Anne in height and weight, a few pills, and five thousand dollars in cash. They drove to the house together and parked behind the garage.

When Anne first saw Bobby, her heart ached as the child was just waking up. When Bobby recognized Brad, he called out to him and lifted his arms to be picked up. Brad ignored him. Bobby was now crying and saying, "I want Mommy." Anne nearly fainted as she recalled the many times she had calmed Matt when he cried for his missing mother. Without any more hesitation, only empathy and love for the boy, she picked him up, cuddled him, and whispered comforting words into his ear. "Hi, sweetheart. I'm going to take care of you now. We will have lots of fun."

He turned to look at her but was too confused to understand what she meant. It just felt good to be hugged.

Brad quickly packed a bag of Bobby's clothes, threw in some toys, and finally told Anne to put the still-sleepy child in the car.

Bobby started crying while being led from the house to the car, so Anne took a moment to soothe him again and promise a nice long car ride. She gave him some of the treats she found in the car. There were also a few toys around his car seat.

"Will you hurry up," Brad called from behind the door. He had not followed them out. He wanted to avoid being seen by the nosy neighbour, Ralph Cornwallis.

Once Bobby was strapped in, Anne placed his suitcases in the trunk of the car and drove away. She was still a novice driver so took extra care negotiating the car out of the driveway.

\*\*\*

It was nearly five o'clock on Friday when Frank's receptionist buzzed to say that Flo Johnson and Mary Andrew were here to see him. *Well, what was a pleasant surprise,* he thought. He immediately reached for his wallet and wondered what society or charity they were collecting for this time.

He stretched his legs and got up with a big smile to greet them.

"Well, hello, Flo, Mary. It's always a pleasure to see you and contribute to whatever endeavor you are currently supporting. Now let me see, your own children have long ago quit being involved in amateur sports and school activities. Oh, I get it. Your grandson is now the focus of your fundraising. How much is this going to cost me?" he chuckled.

When there was no response from either lady, he looked a little closer at them and noticed they were visibly upset. It did not take long to realize that they were not there for a donation.

"My goodness, ladies. What is it? What's wrong?" he queried.

Tripping over each other's words, they blurted out a barrage of information and a demand that a missing child bulletin be issued for Monika Andrew and four year old Bobby Andrew.

"Whoa, ladies, calm down, speak slowly and one at a time. Flo, you go first."

"Every day at twelve-thirty Monika phones me and I chat with her and Bobby. But today, when she hadn't called by one o'clock I phoned her. Instead of her or Bobby answering the phone, an automated voice came on saying that the phone was no longer in service. That was really odd, so I phoned Brad at the office to see what could be wrong with the house phone. His office phone went to voice message, so I phoned Mary."

By now, Flo was too agitated to carry on. She was tripping over her own words. She stopped to use a tissue and dab at her eyes, so Mary took over the story.

"Well, I also thought it was very strange, so I called Brad. I phoned the business and got a recording. So I phoned my daughter Kristie. According to her, Brad had only been in the office for about an hour before lunch and had asked not to be disturbed. He had just returned from his visit with the doctor, locked himself in the office, and then left around ten o'clock, returning around two o'clock. A customer was with him. He told her and Mark to leave for the day. He seemed distracted and didn't even ask how the day was going."

Flo took over again. "I phoned Mandy to ask her if she knew where Brad, Monika, and Bobby could be. She said they were planning a weekend away to relax and hopefully conceive a child. I was thrilled because we knew they had been talking about enlarging the family. But they wouldn't leave town without telling us."

Neither woman had been able to locate Brad or Monika. They were worried they had all been in a car accident. Frank promised to look into it but felt there was nothing to worry about. Besides, it really was too early to issue a missing child bulletin as there really was no evidence anyone was missing, other than the fact that a phone did not work.

But he did call in Sergeant Clyde Michaels. "Clyde, can you take down some information from these ladies and then see me."

Fifteen minutes later, Sergeant Clyde Michaels reentered the office with the name, make, and licence plate number of Monika's car and Monika's and Brad's credit card numbers.

"Good work. Now can you phone the hospitals and neighbouring precincts to see if any accidents involving the car have been reported and check for activity on the cards?"

At quitting time, instead of going directly home, Frank started his own inquiries. He could not locate Brad, and as the ladies had said, he was not answering his phone. So he drove to the Andrew's house. No one was home, and there was no sign anything was out of order. Even old Mr. Ralph Cornwallis was sitting on his deck watching everything as usual. The two men exchanged waves as Frank returned to his patrol car and drove off.

At home that night, as he was pondering the strange story, Frank's wife called him for dinner. As he often did, he shared his day with his wife. When he told her about the strange visit from Flo and Mary, his wife Coralee had some information for him. She happened to see Brad that morning, sitting in his car in front of the clinic. He appeared to be in great distress and was pounding the steering wheel and shouting.

Frank decided that might be a clue worth following up on. Had Brad been to see a doctor, and if so, had he been given bad news?

# CHAPTER SEVEN

# SPRING 1995

After Anne drove away on Friday, Brad touched each of his trophies, caressing his favourites and remembering accurately the day he was presented with each. He checked to make sure the suicide note was still visible on the monitor of the home computer, then toured each room in the house that had been his happy home for five years. He drove around town revisiting the places of his successes. Eventually, he wondered where to go. As he drove near his parents' home, he saw Monika's family hanging around with his own. He quickly pulled a U-turn to avoid any confrontation. He drove up an old logging road and sat for hours, numb. Early in the morning, he snuck into his parents' home and went into his old bedroom. His mom had never changed it. He curled up in a fetal position and started muttering. The noise woke his parents. They came into the room to find a near comatose Brad. They immediately tried to rouse him by shaking his body and firing questions at him.

"Brad, what in the world is happening? What has you so sad? Where are Monika and Bobby? We're all going crazy wondering what's happening!" said his dad.

"Brad, please say something," his mother continued. "Are you hurt? Why did you close the business and send Kristie and Mark away? Who was in the office with you? Tell us, please, the truth cannot be worse than what we and Monika's parents are envisioning. Please, Brad, I can see you are agitated. Did Monika take Bobby somewhere as a treat? Were they in an accident? If so, did you witness it? Please tell us something. We are your parents; we will always love you no matter what. Nothing you can say will change that."

Brad stirred and with glazed eyes said, "They are gone," then rolled onto his other side away from them.

"Joe, do you think we should phone the doctor or Detective Carson?" asked Mary.

"Let's wait and see what happens when he wakes up. It's three in the morning."

All weekend, Brad kept a low profile, only leaving his room for frequent trips to the bathroom, where he flushed the toilet repeatedly. Mary feared that he was throwing up, but he ignored her inquiries. Both Joe and Mary tried to talk to him about Bobby and Monika, but he was mute. His face and body showed no emotion at all. Mary noticed when she went into his room that all the pictures of Monika had been taken down. Was that was what he was flushing down the toilet? No amount of coaxing would move him.

The weekend ended with no hint as to the whereabouts of Monika or Bobby. No accidents had been reported. There had been no activity on her credit or debit cards. If anyone did ask Brad about his family, he simply muttered, "They are gone."

A missing child bulletin was finally issued to beef up the search for Monika and Bobby.

Detective Carson sat at his desk driving himself into a fit as he was unable to make any sense of the missing mother and son. He needed a break. That's when he spotted yet another handwritten letter from seventy-year-old Ruth Wilson. He actually snickered as he reached for the envelope. It would be a welcome diversion. Ruth was the town's watch dog and often wrote letters to the mayor, the paper, and to him. *Wonder what's bugging her now*, he thought. The letter was dated Friday and had been hand delivered as usual.

*Dear Frank*

*Today on my daily power walk up the service road, I stopped to make a pit stop. I walked into the bush and was about to squat when I heard noises. I cowered behind the shrubs and watched. A man had opened the tailgate of a truck and threw a few small bags into the ravine. Next, he tugged what was obviously a heavy hockey bag out of the truck. By now he was sweating so he took off his shirt and tossed it onto a shrub. He heaved the heavy bag and some large metal items into the ravine. I was about to confront him but soon surmised by his expression and body language that he was in a foul mood. Incensed, I took out my camera and took pictures of him and his truck. Then I made notes and sketches on the notepad I always carry with me. My film is at the drug store being developed. When the truck was empty, he grabbed his shirt, leaving a string of it behind. After he tore out of the area, I started to take pictures of the tire tracks and string. Please identify and fine the person in these photos. He has*

*disrespected the environment and should
be shamed into cleaning up his mess.*

*Yours, Ruth Wilson*

The sketches clearly showed a man throwing many items into the ravine. The sketch also clearly identified Brad Andrew's company truck.

Despite the fact that it was the end of a shift, Frank immediately paged all pertinent personnel to assemble in the conference room.

While the groups were arriving, Frank quickly dispatched Sergeant Clyde Michaels to the ravine to set up police security tape. Next, he addressed the assembled group of curious professionals from the constables to the forensic teams.

"Thank you for your speedy response. You will not be going home early today." Once the groans were over, he continued. "As you are aware, this past weekend we have been monitoring the possible whereabouts of Monika and Bobby Andrew. Unfortunately, we may have some very disturbing news."

He then read Ruth Wilson's letter. The silence in the room spoke for itself.

Frank then instructed each team what their role would be once at the site. Although unnecessary, he cautioned everyone to document their every move with photos and notes.

Detective Carson then rushed to the scene. The police tape was already up with officers standing by to deter the press or any onlookers.

Assessing the scene quickly, Frank realized that because of the steepness of the ravine, the Search and Rescue crew would have to be put into action.

The captain of the local search and rescue soon had his team ready to repel down to the bottom of the ravine. While they prepared, the rest of the officers busily collected evidence. The thread described by Ruth was photographed, placed in a bag, and labeled. Other officers were making a plastic cast of the tire tracks.

By now the Search and Rescue team was ready to descend into the ravine. There were four men negotiating their way down with a stretcher and a large canvas bucket. They carefully photographed everything, and then began loading the items on the stretcher or in the bucket. First came the heavy hockey bag and larger pieces of metal on the stretcher. Word was given to pull it up to the top. Next, the smaller items were placed into the bucket. Before it was raised, they made a final comprehensive search for any other pertinent objects that could be of significance. Then they gave the word to raise the bucket before being pulled to the top themselves.

As soon as the stretcher and bucket were on level ground, Detective Carson slowly unzipped the hockey bag. His stomach heaved as he recognized the body of young Monika Andrew. As Sergeant Michaels recorded his movements, Detective Carson slowly turned Monika's body over, wondering as he did if young Bobby would be underneath. With a sigh of relief at not finding the boy, he continued to inventory the other items in the bag—a purse and various framed family pictures that had been smashed.

The forensics team took over itemizing and fingerprinting the large metal objects that were also on the stretcher.

The coroner took over possession of the body as Frank moved on to examine the contents of the bucket. Once again, his movements were recorded. He identified a suitcase containing items of clothing and toiletries common for a woman to pack. The other suitcase contained clothes, toys, and toiletries suitable for a five-year-old boy. Smaller pieces of metal were also processed.

Because of the time of the day and the implication of a serious crime, Frank decided to continue the investigation in the morning. First, the body would have to be formally identified by the next of kin. All members of the investigation crew returned to their respective offices to begin creating a paper-trail of everything that was seen and done. These notes would help them with any resulting trial.

Frank sent an officer to the drug store to pick up Ruth's photos. Since the photos clearly showed Brad was the one dumping the bags, there was no hurry to proceed. However, Frank did assign an officer to locate Brad and to make sure he didn't try to leave town. Sergeant Michaels had located Brad at to his parents' home.

The cause of death would be known by morning. Frank resigned himself to a sleepless night as countless scenarios raced through his mind. How could a seemingly perfect young family come to such a devastating end?

\*\*\*

Dr. Murdock, the coroner, was on the phone.

"Good morning, Frank. The preliminary results show that the victim died of a drug overdose. All of the bruising was post-mortem. I cannot say if it was an accidental overdose or a suicide. Oxycodone was the drug identified."

Based on the evidence already collected at the ravine and the pictures by Ruth, a judge issued search warrants for Brad's truck, his office, the entire demolition yard, and the house.

Brad, as Monika's legal next of kin, was driven to the morgue by the officer that had watched him overnight. It was his responsibility to identify the body.

When they arrived at the morgue, Dr. Murdock lifted the blanket covering Monika's remains. Brad barely glanced at the body, and in a monotone voice declared, "I have absolutely no idea who that is."

With that, he quietly turned away and was about to leave. However, he was detained by the officer and led to an interrogation room at the precinct. He made no effort to resist.

Detective Carson was stunned by Brad's behaviour. He then notified the Johnsons, who collapsed in despair as they viewed the battered and bruised body of their lovely daughter.

The forensics teams were gathering crucial evidence from various locations. Items were catalogued and removed from the house, the truck, the scrap yard, and the office. Hours later, the detectives and other officers sat around the table of evidence.

From the demolition yard, they had collected: an inventory list of items in the police locker with a note from the on-scene officers about missing drugs and money—no such list could be located for the lost and found; tire tracks from the truck; and metal objects matching those found at the scene.

From the truck, they had: the torn shirt; soil samples from the tires.

From the house, they had collected: a computer with a suicide note—only Monika's prints were recovered from the keyboard; and a small bag with traces of Oxycodone but no prints.

Finally, from the ravine, they had collected: a hockey bag with Brad Andrew's name on it with Monika's body inside; a thread that matched the shirt from the truck; tire tracks that matched Brad's truck; large metal items that were logged as belonging to the scrap yard; suitcases filled with clothing and toiletries for Monika and Bobby; and a smashed purse.

The evidence only proved interference with a body. There was no proof Brad had forced Monika to take the drugs. But the biggest mystery was: where was young Bobby? The letter on the computer was the only clue.

*Dear Brad, Mom, Dad, and Mavis,*

*For too long I have lived a life of deception. Today Brad will find out that Bobby is not his son. I cannot live with the disgrace, disappointment, anger, and mystery that will surround all the people I love. I am bringing Bobby to his father and leaving you all forever. If you can ever in your hearts forgive me, I will know. With so much love and guilt and shame, I say goodbye.*

*Monika*

Frank drove to the Andrews' house. Old Ralph Cornwallis was again sitting on his deck, watching everything.

Before going into Brad's house, Frank walked over to chat with Ralph, who was sitting in his favourite deck chair. His coffee cup and newspaper were in hand. Frank knew that people who sit around all day often have pertinent observations to share.

"Hi Ralph" he greeted the man, "How are you doing?"

"Well, Frank, I'll tell you, I'm a little confused," he answered. "I've lived her nearly fifty years. I built this house myself. Raised four children here and lost my wife a few years ago. Over the years, there have been many families in the house next door. But the young Andrew family is by far the best. What a lovely family. Whenever Monika baked cookies, young Bobby brought six for me. Lately, he's been allowed to come over by himself and stay for nearly two hours every Tuesday while Monika does chores. I've been letting him use some of my tools to make bird houses. He sure is one smart little guy."

"But strange things have happened next door. Now, I love that little family, and Bobby, well, I love him like a grandchild. Today, or was it yesterday? Things seemed just a bit different. Brad came home just after ten. He left about an hour later in a hurry. Now, he often comes home for a mid-morning coffee but this seemed different as he parked out of sight at the back door instead of right in front of the house."

Ralph paused and looked pensive for a moment. He took a sip of coffee and looked around. "But the weirdest thing was that around dinner time, I'm sure it was Friday, or maybe Thursday, something else slightly out of the ordinary happened. Monika, wearing a big floppy hat, put boxes into the trunk of the car. Bobby was crying, a rare occasion as he was always such a happy boy. Then she drove off without the usual honk and wave."

*Well*, thought Frank, *that somewhat fits in with the weekend away Mandy mentioned. But this old guy seems pretty confused about what day this happened.*

He thanked Ralph and went into Brad's house. Frank wandered from room to room, searching for some kind of divine intervention to help him understand what had happened.

\*\*\*

Back at the station, Brad still did not appear aware of his surroundings as he was led back into the interrogation room after a bathroom break.

Just as they were going through the door, a commotion erupted in the outer office. Joe Andrew came running down the hallway demanding to see Brad and find out what was happening.

"Frank, in the name of all that is holy, what are you doing? Brad, are you alright?"

Sergeant Clyde Michaels immediately stopped Joe from grabbing Brad, who seemed unaware of his father's presence.

Detective Carson quickly responded by talking quietly to Joe. "Relax Joe; we just need to talk to Brad about the death of Monika and the disappearance of Bobby."

"Not without a lawyer. Wait until I get in touch with Harry Nichols before you begin. He looks after all our legal issues with the family and with the business. I want him to be here."

Detective Carson knew that Brad had a right to have a lawyer present, so he locked Brad in the room and went back to his office to go over his notes.

An hour later, Harry Nichols arrived at the station.

Joe, who was in a state of mixed emotions—anger, confusion, denial—was hardly coherent. He paced the floor, wiped his brow and tried to get Brad to speak.

"Brad what happened that is so awful that you can't speak. Who hurt Monika? Where is Bobby?"

Brad had not moved or spoken, but seemed to be in a near catatonic state.

Once the men were seated, Harry began. "Good afternoon, Detective Carson. Can you inform me of the charges and the evidence against Brad? As you can image, the town is abuzz with all sorts of stories. Let's start at the beginning of the timeline you've established."

Frank gave Harry a brief recap, then began the interrogation. "Brad, do you know why you are here?"

Brad gave no answer or response of any kind. This was to be the pattern for most of the interview.

"On Friday, you were very upset after seeing Dr Tait. Can you tell us why?"

Silence.

Frank took a moment to collect his thoughts. *The suicide note gives us motive. Now we must find out what she did every Tuesday afternoon.* It would be a query for another time. He added this thought to his notes then carried on with the interrogation.

"Brad, after you left the clinic, you went to your office, where according to Kristie, your sister and office manager, you paced and cursed and demanded to be left alone."

Brad simple stared straight ahead.

"About thirty minutes later, according to your employee Mark Hunter, you drove your pickup to the scrap heap and loaded a few pieces of metal into the truck."

Frank was met with more silence.

"According to your neighbour Ralph Cornwallis, you sped into your driveway and parked at the rear of the house, which was unusual. You later left in a hurry."

More blank stares and silence filled the room.

"Tell me, Brad, was Monika alive when you got home? Was Bobby in the house?"

There was no answer, not even a flicker of emotion on Brad's face.

"Did you kill Monika?"

No response.

"Where did she get the drugs? Did she have access to the RCMP locker at the scrap yard? Do you use drugs regularly? Did Monika? Did you see her suicide note on the computer monitor?

Did you write it?"

More silence.

"Brad, we have pictures and forensic proof that you threw Monika's body into the ravine. Your lawyer can see them here on the desk."

"She's garbage so I threw her out!" shouted Brad.

"What did you say?" demanded Detective Carson.

"Enough Brad" cautioned lawyer Nichols.

"Brad, where is Bobby?" continued Frank.

"Gone," Brad moaned.

"Brad, according to your neighbour, every Tuesday, Bobby went over with fresh baked cookies and stayed for ninety minutes. Can you tell us what Monika did every Tuesday?"

Brad froze then stood up and let out a primitive scream that shook the room. He wailed, "That whoring bitch."

He sat down, once again immobile, but with involuntary tears leaking out of his eyes.

This reaction shocked the three men. Obviously, Brad was unaware of Monika's Tuesday activities. Is that when she met the mysterious father of Bobby, or someone else? It seemed impossible as this was such a small town that a pattern of behaviour like that would have been noticed.

The interview was futile. Brad's only answer about Bobby was, "Gone." Or about Monika, "Bitch." He showed no emotion as Detective Carson showed him the evidence against him. He was then formally charged with interference of a dead body and led to a cell.

The men left the office and Harry began the process of getting Brad released. Harry said he would hire an investigator to follow up on the recently aired missing child bulletin. The police had already published the description of Monika's car with no results. Hundreds of tips had been received but so far none had amounted to a real lead.

Frank continued to sift through the pile of information, trying to make sense of it and clarify a timeline.

Just after 9 a.m. on Friday, Brad was seen upset at the doctor's office.

Between 10 a.m. and 12 p.m., he made the trip from the clinic to the office and scrap yard and then to the house before going to the ravine.

Ralph saw Monika and Bobby leave with suitcases around dinner time, but he was not sure of the day.

There were too many questions and not enough answers. If Monika had committed suicide, where did she get the drugs? From Brad's office? Did she know the combination for the police safe? Where did Monika go every Tuesday while Bobby was with the neighbour? If Brad and Monika were planning a weekend away to try to get pregnant, why would she use drugs? Where were the rest of the missing drugs and five thousand dollars cash from the police safe? Who had Bobby, or was he dead?

In the meantime, Joe returned home where he and Mary tried to make sense of the whole drama. Mary was shocked and dismayed to learn that her darling Bobby was not really her grandson. Joe and Mary ended up crying and clinging to each other while trying to absorb how their lives had so quickly and completely fallen apart.

Joe recalled the conversation they'd had with the Johnsons over five years ago when the kids were first expecting a child. The theory was that the child was conceived the first time they had sex. Because the sex was a spontaneous action after the famous basketball game, they did not have condoms.

But if not Brad, then who? The tournament was held in town. There were some out of town teams obviously, but Monika was always with the cheerleaders or with Brad. When did she find the opportunity? Both sets of parents were convinced that Brad and Monika were virgins at the time. The mystery suddenly changed focus.

Is the biological father a local person? Was she still seeing him every Tuesday? Does he have Bobby? Did he ever play a part in Bobby's life? If so, how and when and where?

No matter how hard they tried, Joe and Mary could not find any evidence of trouble between Monika and Brad. They were always so in love with each other and with Bobby. They were perfect parents. What went so wrong five years ago?

\*\*\*

The next day, Brad was released from jail and meekly went home with Joe. Mary had prepared a nice lunch, but Brad just went to his old room and sat in his favourite chair, avoiding any attempt by his parents for conversation.

Meanwhile, the Johnsons were also inconsolable as they tried to come to terms with the loss of their daughter and grandson. Joe had called to tell them that tests proved that Brad was not Bobby's father and therefore their daughter had been unfaithful. The news had knocked them for a loop.

Joe continued. "Any idea who your daughter was with the night of the big game? She was not at the awards ceremony. You will recall how Brad kept looking for her. Who was she with instead of celebrating his victory?"

Doug was so hurt at the accusation that Monika had been unfaithful that he hung up the phone and burst into tears. Flo came running over. In a very emotional state, he repeated what Joe had said about Monika.

Over the years, the Andrew and Johnsons had been inseparable as best friends, but now instead of consoling each other over this tragedy, they were avoiding each other.

The Johnsons had lost a daughter, a grandson, and their very best friends. Pastor Simpson arrived at Johnsons' door using a coded knock so that they knew it wasn't a reporter. They felt relief that there was a non-judgmental ear to listen to their tears. Friends and neighbours had begun phoning or dropping by. One set of neighbours had placed a sign on the Johnsons' door diverting all contributions of food, flowers, and cards to them.

Detective Carson continued his investigation. He re-interviewed Kristie to see if she had any new ideas about the mystery person in the office on Friday. He questioned Mandy to see if she observed any problems in the marriage of Brad and Monika. Once again, he spoke to Ralph Cornwallis but only seemed to confuse the man more. Harry Nichols was also doing some research. He had phone interviews with the former principal and coach from the high school to see if either of them had ever seen an angry or violent side to Brad. No one had. Kristie now hated her brother for making everyone's life a nightmare. She and Mark were also having issues at the salvage yard. She had to hire overnight security as many amateur detectives were trespassing in the yard hoping to find evidence of Bobby.

\*\*\*

It had been a week of rumors in Deer Lake. All of a sudden, people were heard saying they had seen Monika with another man at the park. His description varied so much that the stories soon grew old. Other guys at the bar made comments insinuating that they were the mystery man in her life. People rummaged all through the area around the ravine and at every other isolated places around town. There was even talk of dragging the lake. The Andrew and Johnson families stayed home as much as possible, having friends bring groceries when needed. Brad was still silent.

It was not a quiet weekend in Deer Lake media-wise. A few reporters from different areas had come to town to follow this human-interest story. They interviewed anyone who would talk to them. References were made to studies done about spousal murders. The possibility of a concussion from all the sports Brad had engaged in was also considered. Brad continued being uncooperative about Bobby. A subdued family funeral had been held for Monika. Her parents hired a private investigator to try to find Bobby's whereabouts and to possibly tease out who his father might be or who, if anyone, was Monika's current fling.

A trial date had been set for July 4$^{th}$. Deer Lake was not a big city, so the court docket was not overwhelming. Because both the lawyer and prosecutor said they were ready for trial, the judge streamlined the cases through to clear the calendar for a week. The defense had chosen trial by judge only, simplifying the procedure. Brad still faced only one charge of committing an indignity to a human body.

The missing child bulletin had not resulted in any credible leads. The publications of Bobby's picture were concentrated in BC, Alberta, and Washington State. Sightings were reported in Northern BC and the Vancouver Island and Calgary areas. Not one turned out to be helpful. Some were actually a vindictive parent causing grief for their exes.

Harry Nichols had a team of experts working on research about Oxycodone and infertility, tracking Monika's activities, and following up on every response to the missing child bulletin. Brad was still not communicating. At times he could be heard mumbling but no sense could be made of what he was saying. He had lost a lot of weight but still refused most food. His father had finally convinced him to shower and change. He appeared catatonic most days.

The Andrew family was feeling the full impact of the scandal. On the weekend, they had tried going to the church where they had been active members for nearly thirty years. Some people openly snubbed them, others gave glances of pity, and some came to offer support, but it was all too painful. The Johnsons let out a cry of anguish when they saw them. Kristie and Mavis looked sadly at each other. They realized that their lifelong friendship was over. After the service they left feeling like fugitives. Reverend Simpson was being a great comfort to the Johnson family but had yet to offer support to the Andrew family.

Both sets of Brad's grandparents had arrived in town to offer their support to Joe and Mary. None of them could shake Brad out of his lethargy. In the morning, Mary went into his room to open the windows. She was shocked to see Brad sitting on the floor playing with his long-forgotten Lego blocks. Hoping it was a breakthrough, she sat on the floor with him and asked what he was making. He threw the blocks across the room and curled up in a fetal position.

# CHAPTER EIGHT

# SUMMER 1995

Julia's Diary
Day one: Friday June 2, 1995

I woke up this morning feeling empty knowing it was my last day in Deer Lake—the city where my life was devastated. What to do now? Where to go? I was back to having no family! I did have money but no one to share it with. I had one horrid chore left: go to the police compound, empty the car of personal items, and arrange to have it towed to the Apex salvage yard. How painful it was just thinking about it. How could I possibly be expected to see the death car? Would it be full of the blood of my loved ones? What would I do with the belongings?

I needed to burn off my mixed-up emotions, so I decided to walk the three kilometres to the yard. Once there, I hesitantly entered and stood in the door way. The man behind the desk jumped up and gasped as if he had seen a ghost. He was trembling. When his receptionist came to see what the problem was, he sent her away.

His nametag said Brad so I knew he was the person Mandy told me to see. He composed himself and asked me to sit down. He apologized for frightening me. Then he burst into tears and told me that his wife had left him that morning. She left a note but she also left her son, a boy that up until today, he believed to be his son. It reminded me of how José came to have Matt as his son.

I had no empathy for him, my numbness was complete. When I told him why I was at the office, he immediately recognized my story. He knew I had lost a husband and son. A strange look came over him. He seemed in a trance. He reached for some papers for me to sign, claimed he would take care of the entire matter of the car, then asked if I could come back in two hours. I agreed and went back to the motel to pack my few items. That is where I saw this journal. It was to record the details of a wonderful family holiday. I checked out and walked back to Brad's office.

When I returned, Brad had formed an idea. Without hesitation, he outlined a diabolical plan.

Since we had both lost a spouse and a son, why didn't we even out our karma? I wanted a son; he had a boy he didn't want. Why didn't I take his boy and leave town? My emotions went from shock to incredulity and back to the anger I had felt earlier in the morning. Brad was offering me not only revenge on life but a son to love and the possibility of a future with a family. I found myself agreeing to his bizarre plan.

He went into a safe and gave me five thousand dollars and a woman's driver's licence. We drove to his house and packed his wife's car with clothing and toys for the boy. I carried the groggy child to the car and put him in the car seat. He started to cry for his mom as we drove off. It broke my heart to hear him. He sounded just like Matt used to when he called for his mom.

I drove straight to Rangeland to see my lawyer who had all of my money in trust. Using a bank transfer, we set up an account in Kamloops under the name Julia Anna Novakova. Then I drove to Revelstoke, nearly three hundred kilometres away. That's where my hurdles began. I had to refuel using cash. That meant I had to go into the office. I adjusted my hat and made sure I had sunglasses on. I gave the attendant twenty-five dollars and went back to the pumps. Great! I had never filled a gas tank before. My new son James knew what to do! Next issue was registering for a room at Motel 6.

That was not as easy. The clerk did not like accepting cash. When I insisted, he said I would have to leave two hundred dollars in cash that would be refunded when he checked the room for damage when we left. Fine. He wanted my driver's licence and the car licence. I could see the car from the window but gave him a number that was one digit different. If an alert was ever issued for Monika's car, the number I gave would not be recognized, even if the car description would. My driver's licence was accepted. We walked across the street to a fast-food place. James barely ate anything so I let him spend time in the play area. He kept asking for his parents. I tried convincing him that we were playing a trick on his parents and that is why I was calling him James and he could call me MaMa. Back at the motel, we watched TV.

When the program was over, I told him to get ready for bed. That is when I noticed the fairly new scar on his leg. When I asked him about it, he got really excited as he told me the story.

"I fell and cut my leg and blood was everywhere. Mom wrapped a towel around my leg and we went to the hospital. I was crying really loud. Mom was crying too. Then the doctor put a hose into me and mom, and I got some of her blood. I got six stitches."

I hugged him and told him he was very brave.

I checked the scar over and was pleased to see that it had healed beautifully. We talked a bit about our cuts and bruises until he eventually fell asleep.

There is no news from Deer Lake about a missing child.

Many mixed emotions are guiding me on this new journey—sadness, anger, fear of abandonment, and hope for new a life. But the one thing I don't feel is remorse at accepting a child as a gift.

Day 2: Saturday June 3, 1995

James and I were up early and ready for breakfast. He was still confused and upset. When we got back to the motel after eating, the office was still closed. Should we wait to get the two hundred dollar deposit back or drive off? What action would bring less attention? I decided to drive off hoping I hadn't been recorded on video. I was pretty sure he would just pocket the money and not say a word to anyone. I just kept driving, stopping once in a while to let James run around to burn off his energy and confusion.

At one of the parks, there was a flea market set up. As we wandered about, James spotted a Superman cape. I got that for him and a wig for me, thus giving both of us a bit of a disguise. We drove all the way to Strathmore, Alberta.

Once again, I had to gas up and find a place to stay. Getting fuel was no issue and I was prepared for the motel to balk at cash. When I signed in, I had my driver's licence handy and the incorrect licence plate. But he threw a curve at me. He wanted the deposit plus a copy of the licence. Panic almost hit me. What if he checked the name? Well, no reason to unless I left a mess or caused a problem.

After yet another fast-food meal, we were back in the room watching TV. James was happy in his Superman cape, so we played a bit of pretend. At bedtime, he was once again upset. I read one of his books to him and he finally fell asleep. There is still no news from Deer Lake.

It has been thirty-six hours since I drove off with James. I'm feeling less abandoned and more hopeful. I still fear detection, especially when I see a police cruiser. I am exhausted but still feeling no remorse.

Day 3: Sunday June 4, 1995

I woke up with a sense of accomplishment this morning. For someone who had never read fiction, watched much TV, or gone to movies, it seemed I was born to live a life of deceit. I knew to keep under the radar by not drawing attention to myself. Somehow, I knew what information to conceal, to stay out of sit down restaurants, and to be a comforting parent. I was truly amazed at myself.

By now, I was becoming concerned about the car. It had BC plates and we were in Alberta. I needed to figure out how to get rid of it but still have transportation. Once we checked out of the motel—and made sure the clerk shredded the copy of my licence and returned the money—we were on our way. James was very tired from two restless nights. I knew he would fall asleep in the car as we moved on.

As we were leaving Strathmore, I saw a Walmart and decided to purchase some fresh produce, milk, and cereal to have better food choices. As I was leaving the store, I saw a small RV with a For Sale sign asking for one thousand dollars cash. It was the perfect solution. No more motels or restaurants. Not more BC plates. It was so simple. The price even included all the linen and kitchen supplies! The owner and I walked over to the insurance broker inside Walmart to change the registration and get insurance. Once again, the false licence was not questioned, nor was using so much cash! I moved all of our belongings to the RV, then wiped down the car and left the keys on the front seat, hoping it would be stolen soon. I knew that if it was discovered, the ownership would be traced. It was something to worry about.

For an inexperienced driver, I was doing great with the RV. We drove for a few hours then stopped at a park to make lunch and run around. What freedom! James seemed happier and appeared to be enjoying our little cross-country jaunt. He even started calling me MaMa once in a while.

We drove all the way to Gull Lake, Saskatchewan. I'm no longer worried about having an out of province vehicle, as it's a recreational vehicle and is expected to be traveling. I pulled into the Antelope Lake Regional Park. Cash was easily accepted. I was soon surrounded by helpful advice on how to park. At first it agitated me until I was told it was a normal response to a new arrival.

Once we were set up and dinner was enjoyed, I let James go to play with the other children while wearing his Superman cape. It was hard to keep an eye and ear on him to be sure he did not say anything that might raise curiosity. As I watched anxiously, I chatted briefly with some of the other parents.

Once inside the RV, we played a game of checkers, thanks to the former owners who left behind some games and books. Once James was asleep, I checked my cash. I had left with three thousand dollars from my own account plus the five thousand dollars from Brad. There is still plenty left despite the cost of the RV and insurance. There is still no news from Deer Lake and I'm beginning to feel very satisfied with my adventure to a new life.

My fear is diminishing. I'm a mother. I have a son. And I have money!


Day 4: Monday June 5, 1995

Maybe it was exhaustion or the fresh air or the quiet of the park, but James and I both had a long sleep. We woke up and decided it was time for a shower. We could use the park facilities or our own little bathroom. What great fun learning to use our own shower. Oh, it felt so good! After a healthy breakfast of cereal and fruit we emptied the holding tanks as per instructions, and helpful campers and headed for the highway. What a great start to the day. Before heading out, I took one last look at the news. No news! But we were two time zones ahead of BC.

As we drove, I got him interested in noticing the scenery. We played I Spy. I'm beginning to relax. James seems to be totally distracted by being in the RV. He actually laughed as he discovered all sorts of drawers and cupboards to explore.

The weather was cooperating, making driving easier. I was enjoying seeing so much of Canada. The prairie countryside was a new vista for me. Now I was content, cheerful, and hopeful. What a change a weekend without drama had made. Do I dare assume I could be happy? Swift Current, Moose Jaw, and Regina were all names I had heard so many times and now I was thrilled to be passing through them. By staying on the highway, I was able to make good time. We stopped at a few roadside sites for lunch and play breaks. We arrived at Qu'Appelle, Saskatchewan.

I registered at the Echo Valley Provincial Park just outside of the town. It was so beautiful with sandy beaches, a playground, and fire pits. Wow, it finally feels like a holiday. I hooked up to a full service site so we did not have to worry about the tanks. After dinner and a walk along the beach, we played games and turned in for the night. But first, one last look at the BC News.

All hope for happiness is sweeping away! I had been so naive, gullible, desperate, bent on revenge that I accepted Brad's story without hesitancy! Maybe it was all lies. His wife's battered body had been discovered. Who did it? Brad or the man Monika left with who may be the boy's father? It was a BC story so it was just unfolding. It was all still prefaced by 'alleged.' The reporter promised more news as the police uncover what happened. I feel sick, terrified that Brad is a killer, scared that James and I will be found, worried that I've done the wrong thing. The only certainty is that I won't sleep tonight.

Day 5: Tuesday June 6, 1995

I had a horrible night filled with nightmares. One included me being taken into custody and James calling for his mom. Then I saw myself trying to outrun a police cruiser and crashing, killing James. I pictured myself in jail where all the women hated me for stealing a child. I pictured Brad changing his mind and trying to find us.

There was no way I was capable of driving. What was I to do? I became aware that James was up. He was well rested, thankfully. After breakfast, he sat to watch his favourite cartoons while I went through my options. There were only two. Surrender or keep heading east. At this point, anger returned as did the need for revenge on the world. I was traveling under an assumed name in a new vehicle. I had done nothing to arouse suspicion. So I made the decision to stay one more day at the campsite. I used the time to do laundry and replenish our supplies. Then James and I took advantage of every activity. He loved the lake. I was amazed at what a confident swimmer he was. But it brought memories of his mom teaching him to swim and his grandpa teaching him to fish. The two of us had a wonderful time, sometimes alone and sometimes mingling with other mothers and children. What an amazing actress I am—inside a terrified fugitive, outside a relaxed mom with a happy son.

At noon, I once again checked the news. The information was still sketchy. Monika Andrew was the victim, but no cause of death was being released. But the frightening part was the missing child bulletin for Bobby. How far will the alert be broadcast? Do they know he's with a woman? If so, would every woman traveling with a boy be an automatic person of interest?

By bedtime, the news was really grim. Brad had been interrogated for hours based on pictures taken by a hiker. Obviously, he had said nothing about what happened to Bobby. Was he going to be able to keep our secret? Whatever became of José's car or Monika's car? Would they be clues? I went back to my options to confess or carry on. Once again, the choice was simple.

We had a wonderful dinner of roasting wieners and making S'mores, two things I had only done once with José and Matt.

James fell asleep instantly. I know I will not.


Day 6: Wednesday June 7, 1995

Once we were up and fed, we disconnected our services, waved goodbye, and headed east. For some unfathomable reason, I thought I would be safe once I crossed into Manitoba. Again, I appreciated being in the camper rather than a car. I was very conscious of reading and following all traffic signs. The restless nights and terrible BC news had taken their toll on me. Instead of driving my usual three hundred kilometres, I stopped at an RV park along the Assiniboine River off Highway 1 near Virden. It was built by the Lions Club and looks like a very restful place to recoup.

James seems happy to be parked again. He's getting tired of the constant disruption. I set up and paid for three nights. We need time to relax and bond. We spent time around the facilities and mingled a little with other guests. There was a tense moment when James was telling another boy, Samuel, that his mom was a great swimmer who had taught him how to go underwater. I had just told Samuel's mother that I couldn't swim. Quick on the uptake, she smiled and said "Yes, being a stepmom is not always easy. I know." What a save. Now I could use the stepmom card in any similar situation.

Later, we took the shuttle bus into town to enjoy the local park and to do some shopping. Suddenly, I realized I had lost sight of James in the store. In a panic, I left my cart and started calling for him. I looked behind me hoping to see him. He wasn't there. I hurried back to the aisle we had stopped at while he chose a cereal. He was not there. I fought back tears as I looked up and down each aisle. There was no sign of him. I was nearly on the verge of collapse when I spotted James talking to a store clerk. A range of emotions swept over me; relief that he wasn't lost, fear that he said his name was Bobby, love that my son was fine. Cautiously I approached the clerk.

Once again, I felt panic. What had he told the clerk? When he spotted me, he called MaMa and ran towards me. There appeared to be no doubt in the employee's mind that we belonged together. I offered my profound thanks, acted as normal as possible, and finished shopping. We had plenty of time before the shuttle returned so we enjoyed an ice cream treat. I cannot get over the feeling that Manitoba is the place for us to call home.

It was overall a pleasant day. But I did need to check the news as soon as James was asleep. I did not want him to see pictures of his parents on TV.

Bad news-warrants had been issued for the police to search Brad's home, office, truck, and scrap yard for any leads as to the location of Bobby. There may be no sleep for me again tonight.

Day 7: Thursday June 8, 1995

As I reflect over the events of today, I realize that it was a spectacular day. After breakfast, we made a game of cleaning our little house on wheels. James often made mention of his parents with little observations. "Mom and I always made cookies." "Dad and I played catch." "I miss my mom and dad." I let him reminisce then hugged and tickled him until there was laughter.

I began to wonder how to gently erase his family memories and skillfully instill in him a new reality with me. At first, I told him we were playing a type of Hide and Seek with his parents. But that had run out of credibility, so I started telling him that I was now his new MaMa because his parents had to go away. If I keep the story simple and repeat it often enough, always using the same words, I'm sure he'll accept it.

Once outside, James mingled with the other children. I never let him out of my sight as I pretended to be engrossed in a book.

After dinner, James wanted a campfire.

"Grandpa showed me how to set up the wood to make a good campfire."

"Okay, I said, "Go ahead but I want to light it."

Tired and happy, we came back inside to read a story and get ready for bed. I checked again for news. There was no change in Brad's attitude or any good clues from the missing child bulletin. It was a good day. Maybe I can sleep tonight.

Day 8: Friday June 9, 1995

Thanks to a happy, busy day yesterday, we both slept well and woke refreshed. I felt hopeful that today would be as wonderful as yesterday. We heard about a historical walking tour from Samuel's mom. She and Samuel were going and invited us along in their car. Since they thought of me as James' stepmom, I felt comfortable going with them.

I enjoyed the walk and the comfort of being with other people. After a shower and some dinner, James started yawning. Before long, he was asleep.

There is no new information on the investigation or the missing child bulletin. We had been on the run for over a week now with no problems, but I dare not get complacent.

Day 9: Saturday June 10, 1995

This morning I awoke after a poor night's sleep. James had a very restless night calling for his family. I guess it's because we've been doing a lot of activities that he did with them. I was relieved that he let me comfort him.

But it was moving day and we had chores to do. The only item left that had connections to Deer Lake was the driver's licence I had been using in the name of Abigail Rose Drayton. When Brad gave me the licence, he said that I was the same height and weight as Abigail, but our hair and face shape were slightly different. What if Abigail showed up at the salvage yard looking for it, or would she have already ordered a replacement? It had to go along with the RV. I pondered what to do. Wearing the wig that I bought at the yard sale and wearing large sunglasses had worked so far. No one ever looked at the picture on the licence closely. The agent I dealt with when I bought the RV and insurance barely glanced at it. The motel operators didn't pay much attention. No one asked me to remove my sunglasses. It still remained a potential issue. I had to rely on my continued luck until I could be rid of the RV as that was also in Abigail's name.

By noon, we were back on the highway heading for Benson. Would it be our new home? On the outskirts of town we saw a Walmart. Brainstorm! Would history repeat itself? I pulled into the parking lot and found the old For Sale sign. We went into the store for half an hour. When we came out, there was a young couple with a baby waiting for us. They only had five hundred dollars cash but I told them that would be fine if they would go to the insurance broker in the store right now and complete all the paperwork. They agreed, and before long, James and I were standing in the parking lot with our suitcases. I hailed a taxi and asked him to drive us into town to a motel that was close to the city business area. There was a Motel 6 but I did not want to register in case any of the managers compared notes if the missing child bulletin caught their attention. So we registered at the City Motel.

I am now officially Julia Anna Novakova. My birth certificate was all that I had. The manager accepted it plus cash for one week. James and I are very close to having a home. I just feel it! After settling in, we went to the pool so James could give me swimming lessons. We went to a nice restaurant for dinner, watched TV, played checkers and went to bed. Once he was sound asleep, I checked the BC TV channel but there was no new significant news.

I plan to sleep well.

Day 10: Sunday June 11, 1995

We both woke up a little confused at not being in our RV. After a nice breakfast and shower, we headed out to explore our new town. It was Sunday so all of the businesses were closed. I jotted down the names and addresses of rental agencies, banks, and government offices. It just felt so right being here. We played at a park and had ice cream.

Back at the motel, it was into the pool. No campfire tonight but a trip to a movie theatre. It was a bonding day. The fear is easing. Once James was asleep, I looked through the envelope of documents I had picked up in Rangeland. Luck was with me. In the envelope was a picture ID in my real name on my LPN Badge. Brent had managed that!

That news guaranteed a good nights' sleep.


Day 11: Monday June 12, 1995

James seemed a little distracted this morning. He wanted to know when he would see mom and dad again. I was afraid that if he started crying, I would have to say something to let him know that from now on I was all the family he would have. I agonized over what I could possibly say.

I retold him the simple story that his mom and dad had to go away and I was his family. That did not really seem to work. Finally, I had an idea. I recalled some of the books that I found at the Rangeland Library that I read to Matt about adoption. It explained how his mom was gone forever but José and I were there for him. Tomorrow when we go to town, hopefully I can find a bookstore that has *I Wished for You* by Marianne Richmond and *A Family is a Family is a Family* by Sara O' Leary.

At first, I tried consoling him by concentrating on the present and how much fun we were having on our adventure.

By nine o'clock, we were back in town. The first task was to open a bank account with my remaining cash. I had picture ID and a birth certificate but they wanted an address. I explained that I was new to town and currently staying at the motel. The teller said he would open an account but I would not be able to withdraw money for a few days. Since the bank was a branch of the same bank in Kamloops, I also transferred some of the deposited money into the account. I kept enough cash to get us through the next a few days.

The next stop was the government office to find out the protocols of living in Manitoba. In order to get medical coverage, I need to have a permanent address for three months. That's okay. We are both healthy at present. If we did need to see a doctor, I can pay for the service.

Finally, we needed to find a place to live. I dropped into a RE/MAX office that offered places for sale and for rent. The agent asked if I planned to stay in town. If so, I might be able to buy. It was a buyer's market as a lot of homes were for sale. A new retirement home had opened and many people were selling their small older homes on large properties. Thinking of all the money I had in Kamloops, I said I would consider it.

Together we studied eight properties and shortlisted four. He arranged for viewings.

James and I both liked the blue house on a corner lot. It was already empty. When I told him that I had cash, he wrote up an offer subject to a home inspection and deed search. Wow. It was the karma that Brad had promised. Once I started using my real name, my fortunes were improving. That was enough for one day. James and I played in the pool and walked back to the theatre to see another movie.

A great day indeed. I'm even beginning to believe my own lies. There is no significant news from BC.

Day 12: Tuesday June 13, 1995

Yes, it was a good sleep for both of us. Once up and about, we headed back to town. Everything was okay at the bank. They had checked out my Kamloops account and transferred enough money for the house and furniture. The bank manager was pleased to have me as a customer. I was issued my debit card and credit card.

I wanted to shout out loud, "Hello Benson, Julia and James are home." We went on a shopping spree for new clothes as we were tired of the few that we had been wearing for over a week. Lunch was at a nice restaurant.

The next stop was a driving academy. I applied for instruction saying that I had never had a licence. I was hoping James wouldn't say anything. I signed up, paid with my debit card, and arranged for the lessons. I just needed to find daycare for James.

I had a message from RE/MAX that the title search and home inspection had been arranged.

After a swim and dinner, we played some of our new games. Back to bed and the news channel.

Brad had still only been officially charged with interference of a body. He was out on bail. It looked like my old lawyer Harry Nichols was representing him. He still had not said a word about Bobby.

Perhaps I'll sleep well and even have happy dreams tonight.

Day 13: Wednesday June 14, 1995

It is so nice waking up feeling refreshed and hopeful. RE/MAX phoned to say the deed was clear and the house inspector was pleased with the condition of the home. Once the rest of the money was paid, it would be a done deal. I was advised to get a lawyer to act on my behalf. I had seen a young lady hanging up a sign that introduced her as a new lawyer in town. So I became one of Manjit Singh's first clients.

What a day! James and I went to the Brick and started looking at furniture. Some pieces were immediately available but most had to be ordered in and could take many weeks.

That was enough for one day. Once we had the keys to the house, we could go crazy cleaning it and buying absolutely everything we would need.

It was such a busy day and yet a short entry in the journal. My brain is having trouble keeping up to my actions. The day seemed to go by quickly.

Thanks to the pool, we once again had a pleasant evening.

Yes, I should sleep tonight.


Day 14: Thursday June 15, 1995

I feel my transition is now done. In a week I will be living in my house, making a home for James and myself. I have been Julia Anna Novakova, Anne Novak, Anne Lopez, and Julia Anna Lopez, and now the circle is complete. I am Julia Anna Novakova.

I have a son, James Mathew Oates, who relies on me and will soon love me as his only family.

This journey and journal are done. I will save it just in case . . .

# CHAPTER NINE

# SUMMER 1995

It was July 4th and Gino Cecconi was feeling great. He had spent years working as a lawyer, then as a prosecutor, without ever having a case that caused a media frenzy like this one. Finally, his name may be known— hopefully it would be spelled correctly! He was happy to have Harry Nichols as the defense attorney. There would be no dramatic scenes, all of his evidence would be well researched, and his information would be presented in a formal, professional manner.

The only disappointment was that this would be a trial without a jury, which meant it would be fast but it would lack in drama. The entire province and legal community were watching this story.

Gino had flawless evidence to present so the case was not hard to solve. It should be a slam dunk. He was, however, experienced enough not to be overconfident, so he and his staff continually reviewed the evidence and the list of witnesses to testify about Brad's behaviour on the day of the crime.

Speaking of which, the town was overwhelmed with media presence. Radio, TV, and print reporters were all settled into motels. Tents had been set up on public property to house the cameras and other essential tools of the trade. The reporters were ubiquitous in the town, interviewing anyone who would talk to them. The major players in the drama were extremely uncommunicative, responding to questions with "no comment." The police tape around the homes and businesses of the Andrew family had finally been removed but the hoard of media personnel continued to surround and harass the families to the point that injunctions were filed to protect their privacy. The Johnsons had hired a security firm to guard the house where the alleged crime took place against looters and curious folks. Even the high school was inundated with overzealous reporters and would-be biographers. Eventually, the principal had to get a judge to enforce a no trespassing rule for the school property.

\*\*\*

Judge Margo Farnsworth adjusted her robe and took one last look at the case that was next on the agenda. It had taken years for her to be assigned to the bench.

Margo began life on one of the big ranches in the rural area north of Deer Lake. The oldest of seven children, she learned at a young age how to be responsible by minding siblings, the garden, and the hens. Her parents struggled to make the ranch able to support the large family. There was no extra money. Luck for the family changed drastically due to a winning lottery ticket. There was enough money now to pay off the mortgage, buy new equipment, and hire some workers. But the best bonus of all was there was money for post-secondary education. As the oldest, Margo was first to attend university.

Once finished law school, Margo was immediately offered an entry-level job in the most prestigious firms in Kamloops, Kelowna, and Vancouver.

For years she worked long hours researching, investigating, and preparing well documented evidence. Her reputation and her constant upgrading of her skills caught the attention of the legal community. She became a circuit judge after fifteen years of being a defense lawyer. Five years later, she became a sitting judge in the Deer Lake District.

So far, the cases assigned to her had been fairly simple. In theory, this case appeared simple, but she knew it was anything but because of the notoriety that it had produced. This case would at least get her name in the news!

Harry Nichols had been granted a psychological exam for Brad. Other than some anger management issues, everything came back normal. Brad was competent to stand trial.

"Okay," she thought aloud, "Let's get started." She made her way out of the chambers and into the courtroom.

Once everyone was seated, Judge Farnsworth explained in detail the charges against Brad, what they meant, and what the consequences could be. "Bradley, do you understand these charges?" she asked

Brad showed no sign of understanding what was happening, so the Judge repeated, "Bradley Andrew do you understand that you are charged with committing an indignity to a human body, specifically your wife, Monika Andrew?"

Brad had continued to stare straight ahead vacantly until the he heard Monika's name. That seemed to affect him, and he focused directly on the judge. He said very clearly, "Yes, I understand," in a cold, dispassionate voice.

"How do you plead?" the judge asked, but Brad had returned to his hypnotic state.

Thankfully, Harry Nichols was now able to answer on his behalf. "Brad pleads guilty, Your Honour, under extenuating circumstances that we will explain. At this time, we would like to accept the qualifications of all the professional witnesses the Crown will be calling."

Gino Cecconi rose to address the court, adjusting his jacket as he did so. He was full of confidence. His poise, education at a private international boarding school and Ivy League university were evident.

"Good morning, Your Honour. Thanks to Mr. Nichols for accepting the credentials of all the experts being called to give testimony at this trial."

"I will hear all the evidence but keep it as bare bones as necessary," remarked Judge Farnsworth. "First, we will hear the opening statements. Mr. Cecconi, you may begin."

"Your Honour, the province's case against Bradley Andrew is based on solid provable evidence that he did, with premeditation, dispose of the body of Monika Andrew. We have a motive-his wife had been unfaithful. We have opportunity- he was seen locking his office and driving off. We have a witness that saw him disposing of the body. We have forensic evidence confirming all of the evidence, and we have his confession."

"Thank you, Mr. Cecconi. Mr. Nichols, you may speak now."

"Thank you, Your Honour. We acknowledge that Brad had motive and opportunity and that there is plenty of solid evidence against him. But we need to look further into the psychology of the shocking news that he received. Feelings of betrayal killed all the love he ever had for Monika. His behaviour was rash and violent, but there is room for compassion and understanding when we examine his actions."

Cecconi's first witness was Detective Frank Carson. Frank was seated and sworn in before stating his credentials for the record.

"Detective Carson, I would like to establish a timeline of your investigation. When did you first become aware that there may be a problem at the home of Brad and Monika Andrew?"

"On Friday afternoon, Mrs. Andrew and Mrs. Johnson, parents of Brad and Monika, came to my office to tell me about the uncharacteristic absence of Monika and Bobby. Monika was not answering a scheduled daily phone call from her mother. The ladies conferred with each other by phone. They both tried to phone Brad at the office but there was no answer. They phoned the house again and were told by an operator that the phone was out of order. So they drove to the house and saw that Monika's car was gone. I explained that it was too early to assume they were missing, but just to be sure, I had a sergeant phone the hospitals in the area to see if they were admitted. I also had him check for action on credit or debit cards in Monika's name."

"Did you hear anything at all on the weekend?" asked Gino.

"No, there was no news until Monday morning when I read a note from Ruth Wilson that had been left in my office mail slot."

"Did the contents of that note lead you to the ravine?"

"Yes, as soon as I read the note and studied the sketches in it, I called my team together to immediately get to the ravine area and start the investigation."

"Did you find enough evidence to ask a judge for search warrants?"

"Yes, we searched the Andrew home, the business office and yard, and the truck described in the note." answered Frank.

"Did you bring Bradley in for questioning?"

"We found Brad at his parents' home late Monday and he came without any fuss."

"Can you tell us about the interrogation?"

"Bradley didn't respond to our questions. His father and lawyer were present, but no one could get him to talk."

"Did you then lay the charge of committing an indignity to a human body, namely that of his wife, Monika?"

"Yes, I did. The sergeant led him away to be processed."

"Thank you, Detective Carson. Your honour, I have completed my questioning of this witness."

Judge Farnsworth then addressed Harry Nichols, offering him the right to cross examine.

"Thank you, Your Honour; I have no questions for the witness at this time."

"That being the case, and due to the time, court is adjourned until tomorrow at nine o'clock." Judge Farnsworth pounded the gavel, rose, and returned to her chambers. The courtroom quickly emptied. Members of the media all made dashes to get to their devices to report on the day's activity. The Johnson and Andrew families left quietly, not even acknowledging the close friendship they had enjoyed for so many years. A near catatonic Brad was led from the courtroom by the bailiff.

Gino Cecconi hurried back to his office. He had his secretary order food then reconvened his assistants to once again go over the planned interrogation of the next witnesses, starting with the coroner. He was pleased with his questioning of Detective Carson and was looking forward to seeing how the news reporters would describe the day's proceedings.

Once settled in the conference room, the staff went over all the reports filed by the coroner and the forensic teams.

Harry Nichols followed Joe and Mary Andrew to their home. They also went over the evidence that was presented that day. Harry once again explained why he had not cross examined the detective. It would serve no purpose. Since it was a trial by judge only, there was no point in trying to question any of the evidence. There was no jury that might require clarification of any of the testimony.

When the trial resumed the next day, Gino called Dr. Murdock, the coroner, to the stand.

"Dr. Murdock, you have been sworn in. Can you tell us when you first saw the body of Monika Andrew?"

"At the ravine as it was recovered from a hockey bag."

"Did you examine the body at that time?" asked Gino.

"I did a cursory exam to verify that she was indeed dead. I saw no knife or gunshot wounds, things we usually look for."

"Did you then do a further study at the lab?"

"Yes, further investigation showed that she had died from an overdose of the drug Oxycodone, and all the bruising was post-mortem."

Harry Nichols did not cross examine.

The next witnesses were members on the forensic team. After their testimonies, Gino Cecconi entered the forensic data against Brad into evidence.

Harry Nichols did not object to the items being entered into evidence and did not cross examine.

"Now I will call Ruth Wilson to the stand," Gino said. "Can you tell us what was unusual about your daily walk up to the ravine area?"

"I saw a man empty the contents of a pickup truck into the ravine," declared Ruth in a very confident voice.

"Did you confront him?"

"No, I did not. I took a few photos and made a few sketches to identify the truck and the driver."

"Ms. Wilson, are these the notes, sketches and pictures that you took that day?"

"Yes."

"Thank you."

Once again, Harry Nichols accepted all of the items into evidence and did not cross examine.

It was then time for the defense to explain Brad's case. Even though Brad pled guilty, Harry wanted some more facts recorded into the transcript and made available to the judge.

"I call Dr. Tait to the stand."

Through his questioning, Harry had Dr. Tait disclose how the day had started with Brad receiving disturbing news as a result of tests. But because of doctor-patient confidentiality, he could not tell the court what those results were.

Gino Cecconi did not cross examine. The doctor left the stand.

"I call Joe Andrew." Joe was allowed to answer the questions that the doctor could not due to the existence of the Power of Attorney papers. Harry got Joe to tell the lifelong love story of Monika and Brad. It all came to a halt when Brad learned he was not Bobby's biological father. That news triggered the drama that left Monika dead, Bobby missing, and Brad in a state of shock.

Gino Cecconi did not cross examine.

Since all witnesses had been heard in record time, the Judge asked for closing statements. The prosecution's summation was brief and comprehensive. The evidence proved an iron clad case. The confession of guilt confirmed the evidence was valid.

Harry then gave a possible hypothesis of the events.

"Brad loved Monika for over twenty years. He gave up a promising career to be with her. He loved young Bobby. When he found out he had always been sterile and his blood was incompatible with Bobby's, he drove home to confront his wife. He was prepared for an argument but instead found her dead by the computer. She must have known what he would learn. There was no sign of Bobby. Brad read her suicide note and lost his focus. Not knowing what else to do, he decided to hide her body. If Bobby was already gone, then she could go as well. Perhaps that is why he has been in a dazed state since hearing Monika's secret."

Harry's words sparked an almost imperceptible reaction from Brad. He tensed up and tears welled in his eyes as he recalled that horrible day.

Brad was startled by the judge pounding her gavel. He looked around, not knowing what was happening. The bailiff led him off again. His confusion returned and once again, he was in a dazed state. The trial was over. Everyone left the courtroom to await the judge's decision.

Judge Farnsworth sighed as she removed her robe in her chambers. *Well, that went well,* she thought. *No fireworks, no surprises. Even the reporters looked bored.*

Gino was disappointed with the lackluster case. There would be no rise to greatness thanks to the anti-climactic nature of the trial.

An hour later, Judge Margo Farnsworth called everyone back to the courtroom and proclaimed Brad to be guilty. He would remain on bail until the sentencing hearing in two weeks' time.

\*\*\*

The day after Brad's trial finished, Harry was standing in his office contemplating his career. All current cases were done. The one he was most pleased with was the case of Anne Novak. He had avoided going to court and got her a decent settlement. Maybe now he would take a few days off and go fishing.

Harry was packing his fishing gear into the car when the phone rang. He pondered not answering it until he saw that it was Detective Frank Carson calling.

"This better be important, Frank," joked Harry.

"Yes, it is very important. You may have to postpone your trip. Joe Andrew called from the hospital. Seems Brad had some more Oxycodone pills stashed somewhere. When Mary went to rouse him for breakfast, she found him unresponsive. The paramedics arrived and immediately recognized the signs of a drug overdose. They administered Naproxen before transporting him to the hospital. Brad was pronounced dead just hours ago. I think you'll have some paperwork to do. This case just gets sadder and sadder."

***

The news from BC was broadcast nationwide. Brad had committed suicide. Julia was shocked and relieved. Now her secret was safe. She could keep moving forward.

When Julia purchased her new house, she hired Manjit Singh as her lawyer. The two women bonded quickly. Manjit walked her through purchasing the house and advised her to write a will. The biggest problem was naming a person to take over raising

James if anything happened to Julia. What a conundrum. Who in the world could she possibly name? She had no relatives. James had one set of grandparents but they didn't know where he had ended up. She had no friends at present. Together, they decided to adjust her will in a year when she had time to become friendly enough with someone who could take on the responsibility.

It felt good to be able to talk to someone, knowing the information would remain confidential. Julia was able to tell Manjit exactly how much money she had sitting in a savings account in Kamloops. Money that had been legally acquired. Manjit gave her the name of a local financial advisor, Jack Smithson, who would help her invest the money in solid stocks and bonds. Before she left the office, Julia requested that Manjit hold onto a large box for her. It was not a usual request, but Manjit sensed it was very important to Julia, so agreed to hold onto the box until Julia had a safe place for it. Her suggestion of using a bank vault was not accepted by Julia.

Julia next visited Jack Smithson. He guided her through the steps of building a comprehensive portfolio to guarantee her a generous monthly income and still preserve her current balance of nearly two million dollars.

Settling down and establishing a routine and a sense of normalcy, Julia concentrated on furnishing their home, working in the yard, and becoming friendly with people she saw regularly. Another important strategy was to frequent the same stores and park areas to become known as Julia and James, her son from a previous marriage.

Julia was happy with her purchase of the house. She wanted James to have a place to play and bring friends over. She would also be able to have a vegetable garden and a few flowers. Not wanting to go back to caring for adults, Julia took a short course in early childhood education. With the help of Manjit Singh, she opened a before- and after-school program. It gave James a chance to socialize. Best of all, she would always be on the alert for any breach on his part.

To everyone in the town, she was Julia Novakova and he was James Oates. They had money from an inheritance and an insurance settlement in her name. Since that information was true and confirmed via gossip by the clerks at the bank, she did not have to explain not needing to work full time.

\*\*\*

In September, Flo and Doug Johnson paid off the private detective they had hired to search for Bobby. No useful tips had ever surfaced. Then they sold their house and with their daughter Mavis, went to manage a mission for the church in Africa.

Joe and Mary Andrew signed the business and their house over to their daughter Kristie and her fiancé, Mark Hunter. Together with the Johnsons, they sold the house where Monika, Brad, and Bobby had lived. After years of close friendship, the two couples could no longer stand to be together. Joe and Mary bought a RV and left town.

Harry Nichols helped both couples with all the legal work and was finally able to once again enjoy a clean desk. He donned his fishing gear, left his cell phone at home, and drove to the cabin on the lake.

Detective Frank Carson set up a display in the den of his home with all the leads that had been received about Bobby. He could not let go of the story. Frank was convinced that Bobby was alive. There was still no clue that would lead to his biological father or present whereabouts. Who could the father be? A visitor at the basketball tournament? A local person?

There was one more mystery Frank wanted to pursue, especially after an interesting remark by his wife. After watching him ponder the evidence for hours, she realized he was hung up on the reaction Brad had to the question about Monika's Tuesday routine.

"Well, Frank, believe it or not, women often confide more in a female friend than a husband. Why don't you ask Mandy if she knows what Monika did every Tuesday?"

Bingo! He needed to ask Mandy about the Tuesday ritual. That was the second time his wife had helped him see outside the box on this case.

"Mandy, this is Detective Carson. I cannot let go of this case and would like to ask you one more question."

"Definitely, the whole story still makes no sense to me. What can I help you with?" asked Mandy.

"Did Monika ever tell you what she did on Tuesdays while Bobby was with Ralph?" he asked with bated breath, hoping for a definitive answer.

"Oh, that's an easy one. In the morning, she baked cookies and did the prep for a special meal for her and Brad. Tuesday was date night so she took a long bubble bath and set the mood for intimacy," she explained.

"Oh, good grief. Brad must have thought she met a lover and then, still in the mood, seduced him every Tuesday. I sure wish I had asked you this long ago."

Frank scratched his head and went back to staring at pictures of Bobby. Every year an aged photo of him was generated on the computer program. The photo was distributed in BC and Alberta.

*** 

Frank and Harry were sitting in the den.

"I keep going over everything we have. Nothing says that Brad killed Bobby. Perhaps Ralph did see Monika taking Bobby away in the car. If so, where did she take him? To the father? If not, then who was the woman in the car? Bobby's father's wife? But even so, no news of a family suddenly having a new four-year-old son ever surfaced. I ask the same questions over and over and try to come up with a new theory. The only other thing we don't know is who the mysterious visitor was at the scrap yard. We assume it was a man, but what if it was a woman? Was it a customer coming to reclaim a vehicle or items? Did it have something to do with the developer who wanted to buy the property?" Frank continued to do what he had been doing since the trial. Harry listened politely as he always did.

"So, Harry, tell me what you remember from being Brad's lawyer. Anything new ever come to mind?"

"No sorry, Frank, but we have gone over everything Brad said, every move he made, and we still don't know a thing. But I do dwell on a case that I had just closed the day before the disaster of the Andrew Family. It's my own little mystery. What happened to Anne Lopez?"

"Once the entire affair with the Andrew family had been put to rest I received a phone call from the hospital regarding the forms for Mathew Lopez's organ transplant release. Evidently no one had checked and initialed that they had seen his birth certificate. I do recall that when Anne was about to sign, she did hesitate and point to his name. The hospital could be in all sorts of legal trouble if the boy was processed under the wrong name. I tried locating her. I called the attorney in Rangeland but he had no idea where she was. I do hope she is well.

\*\*\*

Finally, Flo and Doug Johnson were in a happy mood, a rare feeling for them for the past three years. There was not a day that went by that they did not grieve for Monika and question how she could possibly have been unfaithful to Brad. And where was Bobby? At first Mavis, did not want to give up everything and move to a church mission in Africa. But once she realized that staying in their hometown was unbearable, she agreed to accompany her parents. What she could not believe was how much she loved the lifestyle. Helping others was so rewarding, the climate was comfortable.

Soon she was getting married. Melvin Freeman was an awesome man and she loved him as her mom loved her dad. They would marry and stay until the mission was running smoothly then move on to begin another camp. Her parents had gone back to Canada a few times and knew that when it was time to retire, they would return, but definitely not to Deer Lake.

Joe and Mary Andrew had spent three years on the road, moving constantly, trying to out-run the nightmare that life had dealt them. They had had everything: a strong love for each other and the love and respect of their daughter Kristie, their son Brad and his wife Monika, and their grandson Bobby. They had lifelong friends in the Johnsons, a place in the church and community, a thriving business, and good health. Then it was all gone. They just drove until they were tired and pulled over as soon as they saw an RV park or parking lot.

Kristie contacted them a year later to tell them that the same realtor was back offering to buy the business. They gave her their blessing to sell so that she could also leave town. Harry Nichols handled the legal issues. Then Kristie and Mark packed up, met up with Joe and Mary just long enough to get married, and then headed off for a trip around the world for six months. Once back in the country, they settled in Alberta where they bought a tow truck business and decided to start a family. With the last name Hunter, no one would ever associate them with the Andrew scandal that would surface every time Frank Carson issued another age-enhanced photo of Bobby.

*\*\*\**

Life in Benson was going smoothly. In the three years since her brave move to steal a life for herself, Julia had adapted easily to a life of subterfuge and survival. She was shocked at how easy she found it. In the past, she had survived by being invisible but not dishonest.

Having spent her life being low-key and not participating in any form of gossip, holding her tongue was easy. Staying aloof but friendly kept the curious residents at arm's length. She did not realize how good she was at reading people. It helped her weed out a few people who genuinely wanted to be her friend, no strings attached.

James was happy with his new name and his MaMa. He cried less and seldom asked for certain items or people. Julia knew she would have to come up with a plausible cover story someday for when he asked about his dad and why he had no relatives.

After two years, Julia quit taking in children in order to spend more time with James and volunteer at the clubs and activities he was interested in.

Life was good. She loved and was loved. Julia rejected all advances made to her by men so her social life was confined to her son's friend's moms, the friendly neighbours, and her colleagues at the thrift shop where she volunteered.

# CHAPTER TEN

# SPRING 2008

James sat at his desk, staring at college application forms. Academics had come easy for him so his chances of getting into university were great. However, he had no interest in any particular career path. Over the past three years, he had worked part time at a restaurant, a retail store, and a landscaping business. None of which gave him any hint of what direction his life should take. He knew his mother was adamant that he attend university, but it seemed pointless to him to waste time and money taking random courses with no particular goal in mind. Oh well, it was probably too late to submit an application. Some of his classmates had already been accepted to post-secondary institutions so would be leaving town. Some were planning to stay in town, attend the local college, and earn diplomas in blue collar occupations.

James looked around his room. It had been redecorated a few times over the years, but still seemed a bit sterile. He did not have posters of famous people or movies. There were a couple of good citizen awards from middle school and a collage of his birthday photos from six years old. There were no baby pictures. That observation set his curiosity off again, and he wondered why every so often he would remember events that his mother dismissed. Why did she sometimes call him Matthew, his middle name? Why did he react to the name Bobby? Was it really an imaginary childhood friend as MaMa tried to convince him? Why can he sometimes visualize faces of many people not in his life? What he really wanted was to somehow explore his hidden memories. A school psychologist had taught him about repressed and false memories. How can he separate the two with no clues? According to MaMa, the movers had a lost a few boxes of their belongings. But it was odd that there wasn't a single item or picture from his first four years of life.

Whatever, he'd had a good life so far, even if there was no extended family. Over the years, a Big Brother or church member acted as a positive male influence in his life. Other than a man to call Dad, he was better off than a lot of the other boys in his school. He and MaMa lived as a comfortable middle-income family that had the necessities of life and a few extras. They never had a real holiday though. Over the years, they took many car trips, always to the east or north, never to the west or across the border. Whatever, soon, he would find out how to pursue his hallucinations, or bad memories.

It was time to put on his new suit and get ready for his graduation ceremony. He wasn't all that keen to attend but his mother was bursting with pride for him. She bought a new outfit, had her hair done, and was all excited. There was no way could he disappoint her.

The ceremony was, as he expected, long and boring. All the other grads seemed to be surrounded by extended families while he just had his beaming mom.

After all the festivities, picture taking, and visiting were over, they returned home.

James returned to his room to change out of the suit and into his casual clothes. Then he heard a scream and a crash coming from his mom's room. He ran to her room and found her lying on the floor.

"MaMa did you fall? Let me help you up." She did not respond. Maybe she fainted and would come to and wonder what had happened. He touched her face. It was warm. He tried to check for pulse but wasn't quite sure how. He felt himself begin to cry. Never had he see her look anything but confident and healthy. Did she have a heart attack? Was it his fault for stressing her out about not wanting to go to university? Were there symptoms he should have noticed? There was still no reaction when it dawned on him that he should phone 911.

"911 How may I help you?" answered a calm voice.

In a panic filled voice James cried, "My MaMa fell and I can't wake her up!"

"Can you tell by looking at her chest if she is breathing?"

"She's not breathing!"

"I see your address on my screen. An ambulance is on the way. Do not hang up until the paramedics are in the house. Can you tell me your mother's age, any medication she is on, her family doctor's name?"

When the ambulance crew arrived the EMT did a quick exam then placed her on a stretcher and into the ambulance. James was allowed to drive to the hospital with her but was sent to a waiting room as soon as she was in the emergency room. Dr. Westhill, the family physician, had been notified and was there when the ambulance arrived. James paced back and forth. After what felt like hours, Dr. Westhill came into the waiting room to speak with him.

A team of ER personnel had worked diligently, but they were unable to save Julia. She had died instantly of a brain aneurism.

When James heard the news, he shook his head and tried to toss the horrible truth out.

"That can't be true. She has never even had a headache!"

"James, an aneurism is a bulge in a blood vessel. It is a time bomb waiting for the perfect condition to burst. There are no symptoms so they are only discovered when the physician is looking for something else."

Dr. Westhill sat with him at the hospital coffee shop for thirty minutes, letting him talk and vent and grieve. Dr. Westhill eventually drove James home and went inside while he called someone to stay with him. James did not know whom to call. It hit him that he was now alone. He pretended to call someone so he could tell the doctor that a friend was on the way. He needed to be alone with his thoughts.

James was devastated. He had no idea what to do next. For hours, he sat with his racing mind while his emotions jumped from confusion to depression. Now what? Julia was all that he had. There was no go-to person to comfort and guide him. He thought of the people in his life. His MaMa had a few friends, but they didn't seem to be the right fit to help him right now. The small town grapevine had spread the news of Julia's sudden death. Many people had already started arriving at his home. Not knowing what to say or how to respond, he didn't answer the door or the phone. Who could he turn to? The church minister, Reverend

Thompson, was not only the leader of the church, but he and his wife had often been guests in their home. He had knocked on the door a few times and called. Maybe he was the one to turn to. Mr. Carlton, the school counselor, had also been a friend at times. He too had been to the door but received no response.

Twenty-four hours later, James went back to the hospital to see what needed to happen next.

"Good morning James, How late did your friend stay with you? I'm sorry that I had to leave before he arrived. Were you able to get any rest?"

"My friend left at midnight. I think I dozed off a couple of times."

(James could not believe how easily he had lied twice to the doctor. His mother would be appalled at this new behavior.)

"Doctor, I need to know what happens next."

"Your mother had an arrangement with the funeral home so they have taken her to their funeral parlour. As far as anything else, you should contact your MaMa's lawyer to see what directions that she left behind. If you need my help, just call."

James picked up his MaMa's list of business cards by the phone and looked for a lawyer's card. He knew that twice a year, Julia would meet with Manjit Singh, the lawyer, and Jack Smithson, the financial advisor. He never paid much attention to the reason for these meetings. So on Dr. Westhill's advice, he called Manjit's office to make an appointment.

The next afternoon, showered and cleaned up, James entered the four-story brick building on Main Street for his first meeting with Manjit. The directory in the lobby showed her office was on the third floor. Rather than take the elevator, he chose to walk up the stairs. He tentatively opened the office door. It was a typical sterile office, with a receptionist who stood up when he entered.

"Hello, James. Please take a seat and I'll tell Ms. Singh you are here. Would you like a cup of coffee or glass of water?"

James refused a beverage and self-consciously took a seat. Within minutes, he was ushered into the main office. It had a stunning view of the city. The furniture was quite ornate, a contrast to the outer office.

Manjit rose from her chair and walked over to meet him. "James, I am heartbroken for you at the loss of your dear sweet mother. I like to think of her as a friend. I offer you my sincerest condolences. It is so sad that this happened. Now is the time to deal with your next move. Please take a seat and we can begin. I met your mother when she first moved to town. Actually, I had just started my practice and she was one of my first clients. Over the years I have assisted her with various legal transactions. I did, over the years, adjust her will to reflect your age changes."

Manjit then reached over to a large file that was on her desk. She withdrew a folder.

"This is her last will, made just weeks ago when you turned eighteen. Obviously, except for two donations, one to the church and the other to the Children's Society in town that supports single mothers in the area, you are her sole heir. As a result, we can probably skip probate as the transfer of assets should be straightforward."

James was confused. What was she talking about? Had he not been paying attention? How could she have such a thick file on his MaMa? Why did she even need a lawyer? *Stay focused,* he told himself. He asked her to please repeat what she had just said.

"There are many government forms to fill out, but I can take care of that for you. I have all her important information and can easily populate all the forms. I will just need your signature on all of them. You will be eligible for a death benefit from the government."

*Death benefit? What is she saying? I'm to benefit from her death? What sort of relief would that bring?* He felt his eyes tearing but was determined to stay focused on Manjit's words.

Manjit then asked if he was okay and wanted to continue or take a break. James just wanted it done, so took a deep breath and only asked for a glass of water before continuing. He scratched his head and clenched his fist, trying hard to absorb all the information he had been told thus far. He got up, stretched his legs, and gulped the water. Soon he was able to continue.

"Let us continue with the list of assets and how to transfer them to your name. When you turned eighteen, your mom had your name listed as co-owner of the house."

James was shocked by that news, and then he remembered his eighteenth birthday. He had wanted a party with his few friends. MaMa had been reluctant, but in the end, after a minor argument, she relented. But first she asked him to sign some papers. He remembered asking her what they were for. Now he recalled her answer. "Now that you're an adult, I am adding your name to my assets as a partner or a beneficiary." Yeah, like he believed her. But now it showed how much she trusted and loved him.

"Some of the other papers you signed put your name as beneficiary to her investments and as co-owner of her bank accounts. All of these transfers are simply a matter of you presenting a copy of her death certificate and will to the bank, any clerk in the housing department at city hall, and Jack Smithson at his investment firm."

Manjit got up from her desk and walked over to James. He stood up as she took both of his hands in hers. "James, I cannot begin to understand your grief at this time. Julia loved you so much and was always bragging about you. She lived for you." She gave him a hug and added, "Once you have managed all those tasks, come back to see me for the rest of the estate contents. On your way out, make an appointment with Sara for a week from now and we can map out your next options."

Confused about his next move, he did what he always did—ran for hours as his brain tried to sort itself out.

What now? School was over. His MaMa was gone. His friends will soon be gone to pursue careers or education. Reverend Thompson called and dropped in offering his services as a mentor. James was not in any way ready to confide because he did not know what to say.

Seven days later, James was ushered into Manjit's office. He was nervous and confused about what else she could possibly tell him. As she had directed, he had been to the bank, insurance company, and the investment advisor to show his MaMa's will, certificate of death, and his birth certificate in the name of James Matthew Oates. He was still reeling with the discovery of her vast wealth, which was now his.

Manjit greeted him with a handshake and a warm smile. "Have a seat James. I imagine you've had a very busy week. Losing your dear mother was shock enough, but learning what you have over the past week must be even more confusing. I hope you have been able to have some time with Reverend Thompson. He is a gracious man who will let you say or express anything you need. He'll let you cry, shout, accuse, vent, or melt down. Remember, like me, he is bound by oath to keep everything you say confidential."

James made a non-committal grunt, took a deep breath, and blurted out, "The offices I've visited are saying that MaMa was worth over two million dollars. How can that be? She hasn't worked for years. I know she inherited insurance money when dad was killed in a car accident, but that was many years ago. Where did all the money come from? Why did we always live modestly? Why did she insist I have a job starting at age fifteen? Why could we never have a decent vacation?" James gasped for air, covered his head, and sank down into the chair.

"I can understand your shock. The explanation to some of your queries is easy. Due to your mother's ethics and need to be a good parent she wanted to teach you the value of a balanced life. Julia was a humble woman who did not flaunt her wealth. Over the years, she gave anonymous cash donations to various charities. Because of the untimely accident that killed your father, she knew how quickly life could change. If anything happened to her, she needed to know that you would have survival skills, including a solid work ethic. To explain the source of the money I need to add a chapter of her life. Julia received not only the life insurance, but a large settlement from the other driver. Also, she was the sole inheritor of a large estate belonging to a woman she had befriended."

Manjit paused for a while to let James comprehend the news. She straightened up and continued.

"Burdened with so much money, she deposited it in two accounts in Kamloops. All of the money was in bank drafts so it didn't leave a paper trail as to where it all came from. The money that she had was legally obtained so I never did ask why it was so important that she not leave a paper trail. She operated the after-school daycare so she could monitor your social life, not to make an income. Once you were out of primary grades, she turned it over to another single mom who needed it for the same reasons."

Once again, James took an enormous gulp of air. His heart was pounding as it was having trouble keeping up with his brain.

Manjit began talking again. "I have one more item to discuss with you. Years ago Julia, entrusted a very beautiful jewelry box to me for safe keeping. I have no idea what is in it or why she couldn't put it in her bank safety deposit box. She wanted me to give it to you personally at the time of her death. Her only comment was that the contents will change your life drastically. I don't know anything about Julia's past life and I never pried. On a few occasions, she would come to the office, open the box, and remove or add something. Perhaps this box will answer a lot of questions for you."

James stared at it. It was obviously very expensive. It was covered in intricate carvings with the pattern of a flower in the centre. There were diamonds along the stem of the flower. What could be in it? He drew himself up and stared questioningly at Manjit. Her face held no clues. She gently pushed the box towards him - the Pandora Box? James was in no hurry to accept it. His stupor was broken when he realized that Manjit had stood, signifying the meeting was over. She reached out her hand to shake his.

"James, if there is ever anything you need explained further or any legal advice or help please make an appointment to see me. Your MaMa and I were friends and I do miss her."

With that polite dismissal, James picked up the box and, in a daze, brought it to his car. He sat for a few minutes and stared at the box before driving home. He began to think of it as THE BOX.

Once home, he sat in silence trying to decide when to open THE BOX. He was afraid and anxious and curious and undecided. So he did what he always did and went for a run.

\*\*\*

James ran the last block until he reached his home. As usual, he staggered in, gulped down an energy drink, and collapsed on the couch. He closed his eyes and monitored his breathing until he felt better. When he opened his eyes, the first thing he saw was THE BOX.

Decision time: Open it. Leave it for another day. Store it for another time.

The questions about what to do next kept circling in his mind. He was experiencing too many emotions that needed purging. He felt anxiety about how it would change his life; curiosity as to what could it possibly contain; anger that secrets had likely been kept from him; relief that he may finally know the answers to his nebulous memories.

Procrastination was the way to go. Realizing that he had not eaten since breakfast, James scoured the kitchen for anything that could be made into a meal. He didn't really want another pizza. He found eggs, bread, jam, and an apple. Sounded like a balanced meal, so he scrambled the eggs in a pan, toasted the day-old bread, and washed the apple. He ate slowly and absently while staring at THE BOX.

Still putting off the task, he washed the dishes and sat to watch a movie. He awoke at midnight, confused. He looked around the room and saw that the only source of light was the TV. It seemed to shine right on THE BOX.

James decided that he might as well be alert when he finally opened THE BOX. So he had a shower and a shave, changed his clothes, cleaned his teeth, and combed his hair.

Back in the kitchen, he sat down and stared at THE BOX. It really was a beautiful piece of art. But would it answer all his questions or solve all his mysteries?

*Okay, man up. Open it,* he thought. But he couldn't. It was locked. He didn't want to pry the lock open. Manjit never said anything about a key. Then he remembered that MaMa often wore a chain with a key. James ran to her room and searched through her jewelry. It wasn't there. *Think, Think! Right, she wore it to my graduation!* James recalled the envelope handed to him at the hospital that contained Julia's personal belongings. He located the envelope and thankfully, the key was inside.

Absolutely no more reason to procrastinate. He was rested, fed, and clean. James tried the key. Yes, it fit. He opened THE BOX carefully.

The first level was a tray that contained jewelry he had never seen before. He knew his MaMa would never wear such large, garish pieces. Where did they come from?

Under the tray were papers and envelopes. The first item was an envelope that obviously held a card and was addressed to My Dear Son. Below that were several numbered envelopes. He assumed that indicated the order they were to be opened in.

With trembling fingers, he opened the card and withdrew the paper inside. Deep breathe in and deep breathe out.

*My dearest James,*

*You have been my reason for living. I have loved you completely, unconditionally for years. I only hope that you can continue to love me once I tell you that our life together has been based on a very big deception that started when you were four years old. Please open the envelopes in the order they are numbered. The motive may not justify the action, but the story will explain the history.*

*I have robbed you from your true heritage in order to satisfy enormous injustices done to you and to me. Once started, there was no going back. I have devoted my life to you and truly believe what I did was for the best.*

*I do not know what age you will be when I die and you read this, but I beg your forgiveness.*

*Your loving MaMa*
*Julia Anna Novakova.*

James read the letter over and over. What could it all mean? He paced the room, racking his brain. He returned to the table and once again stared at THE BOX.

Envelope one was titled My Story. Tentatively, James opened the envelope and began to read.

> *I was born Julia Anna Novakova to Natalie and Tomas Novakova, Polish immigrants. They were killed in a plane crash when I was very young. My aunt and uncle, Terry and Jake Cerny, inherited the entire estate, including a cash settlement from the accident. They surrendered me to child services and I spent ten years in unhappy foster homes and the last three years of my youth in a stable, caring home. I graduated from high school and spent the next years living in Mama Murphy's Rooming House, working and studying. I graduated from college as a Practical Nurse and began my career. Mama Murphy died of cancer, and because she had no family,*

she left me her estate. It was substantial, including money and expensive jewelry.

Later I married José Lopez and we adopted James Matthew Oates, the son of a friend. José and Matt were killed in a car accident. I was alone again, bitter, angry, stressed, and vulnerable.

When I was released from the hospital, I had to deal with the disposal of the wrecked car at a demolition lot. There I met a very distraught man, Brad Andrew. He told me that his wife had run off with someone and left her four-year-old son behind for him to look after. He had found out that day that he was not the father of the boy. Since it was not the first time I had heard of a mother running off with a lover and leaving her child behind, I believed him.

I told him how I had just lost my husband and son. I began to sob. Brad knew my story as it had been a hot topic in the town.

Brad was silent, deep in thought, and told me that he had a solution to both of our losses. Since he had an unwanted son and I had lost a son, why didn't I just take his boy for my own? No one would ever *be looking for him. Crazy as it sounded, in my state of mind, I agreed. I flashed back to my life in foster care and could not wish that on you. Brad provided me with a false driver's license, cash, a car, and your personal belongings.*

*What followed was a bizarre cross-country escapade as I changed vehicles, trained you to respond to James, and persuaded you to call me MaMa. Nearly two weeks later, we ended up in Benson and started life as you know it. All of the details have been recorded in a diary found deeper in this box.*

*Later, I was appalled to learn via the news that Brad had told enormous lies. His wife had not left with another man but was found dead in a ravine. She had died of an overdose. Brad was convicted of disposing of her body. He later committed suicide.*

*So your birth mother, Monika Johnson Andrew, is dead. It was revealed that Brad was not your biological father. Your real father was never identified.*

*You didn't have parents and I didn't have a son or husband, so we formed a family.*

*I have poured all my love into you.*
*Please focus on your stable, happy child-*
*hood. It was the best alternative for you.*
*Based on a lie but better than the truth.*
*What I did was wrong in so many ways.*
*But it saved us both from living our lives*
*with horrible losses.*

*All my love, all ways and always,*
*your MaMa.*

James reread the letter many times, sometimes feeling sympathy for his MaMa's hard life and sometimes feeling angry that she had stolen his real life. There were still unanswered questions. Why was there no one else in his previous life—aunts, uncles, grandparents, anyone—that could have adopted him?

Both his parents were out of the picture. He had a stepmom who raised him in a safe and loving home.

A run was definitely called for. Two hours later, he returned home to stare at THE BOX. James slowly reread both letters. He would look at the diary later. He opened the next envelope that contained some legal items:

A birth certificate for Robert Bradley Andrew.
A birth certificate for Julia Anna Novakova.
A birth certificate for James Matthew Oates.

A newspaper story of the plane crash that killed
   MaMa's parents.
News articles about Monika and Brad
   Andrew's deaths.
Marriage certificate of José Lopez to Julia
   Anna Novakova.
Death certificates for José Lopez and
   Matthew Lopez.
MaMa's high school and college gradua-
   tion diplomas.

James became aware that he had quit breathing
while trying to process all this information. He tried
to reconcile the news into some sort of context. The
items in the envelope helped confirm her story. He
felt angry that she claimed to love him as her son but
had lied all along about their relationship. How could
she continue on so easily if she had just lost the only
two people that she claimed loved her? How was he
to figure out how to be Bobby? How was he to face
the horrid, grisly fact that his mother may have been
unfaithful and may have been murdered? Would he
ever meet any real relatives?

James realized he was tired of being alone. He
didn't want adult company as that would lead to an
examination of his feelings and position. He headed
to the park hoping there was a game of basketball or

tag football happening. Yes, a few guys he knew were trying to set up a basketball game.

"Hey, James, get over here. We need another player!" yelled Derek.

"Count me in," he answered.

For the next hour, James forgot about his situation and enjoyed the camaraderie of the game. After the fun was over, Derek invited him over to his house to play some video games. It felt good to be normal. As expected, he was invited to stay for dinner, an invitation he gratefully accepted.

Derek's parents, after an initial query into how he was doing, dropped the subject, and the conversation turned to local events and reminiscing about all the years the boys had been friends.

Back at home, James decided not to investigate THE BOX further but to continue to feel normal by reading a book.

\*\*\*

Having spent two days hanging around with Derek—cycling, gaming, and playing at the park—James felt he was able to go back to figuring out who he was.

He reread the two letters. MaMa's confession and life story revealed and explained a lot: the tragedy of Monika and Brad's deaths, the anonymity of his biological father, MaMa's loss of her only loves; the truth behind his vague memories, and the reason why he had none of MaMa's physical characteristics.

Tentatively, James reached for the diary. It gave amazing details starting from her meeting with Brad and relating all of her escapades on her cross-country trip from somewhere in BC to Benson, Manitoba. The particulars were very descriptive, not only of her actions but of her emotions as she convinced herself she was doing the right thing. She had also entered all the information she had gleaned about the search for Bobby. One set of grandparents, the Johnsons, were pleading for any information. A Detective Frank Carson was relentless in his hunt for Bobby, either alive or dead.

Once again, James was an emotional mess. He ran to the bathroom, threw up, cried, and collapsed into a heap on the floor. Eventually, he roused, cleaned up, and returned to the story.

James was slowly coming to terms with other mysteries. MaMa had insisted that he learn a lot of survival skills. He knew how to shop using a budget, cook, clean, and do laundry. For those skills, he was now grateful. He set to work in frenzy, vacuuming, washing the floors, cleaning out the fridge and cupboards, sorting and washing his laundry, and even going outside to wash, wax, and vacuum the car. That's when he noticed the neglected yard and threw himself into mowing, weeding, pruning, and raking.

Before long, Reverend Thompson meandered over to chat.

"My goodness James, you are so energetic today. The yard is looking great. Maybe you should come across the street and clean up my place."

"Not today. Between scrubbing the inside of the house, now the car and yard, I'm too tired to even go for my run."

Reverend said, "Whenever you need to chat, know that I am here for you."

James thanked him and carried on with the last of the yard work.

Physical labour was definitely what he had needed. He realized he had been so busy that he had quit thinking about his next move.

Back inside and wearing clean clothes, James carefully made a grocery list. He drove to the local mall, ate at the food court, and then shopped at the grocery store.

Once home again, he slowly reread every document from THE BOX and the reports from Manjit and Jack listing his many assets.

James had had time to digest all the information. He had shared none of it with anyone, including people like Reverend Thompson, Counselor Carlton, or Manjit, all of whom would have kept the information confidential. He was not ready to receive advice on his next move as he was sure they would all want to offer guidance.

So as MaMa would say, "Make a list of choices. Weigh each choice and make a decision."

As a recent high school grad, he would normally be starting a job, continuing to study at college, starting an apprenticeship, finding a girlfriend, or taking off to see the world with only a backpack and an itinerary that took him to exotic places and crummy hostels.

Well, he didn't need a job or further education. No one knew just how rich he was. Taking off to see the world seemed like the best idea.

Once the decision was made, he started researching what his options were. He decided to use the name James Matthew Oates. First, he needed a passport. That would give him time enough to plan where to go and how to get there. He came across a lot of businesses that offered just such a service. Not wanting to be alone for a while, he signed up for a tour of Asia with Outward Fun Tours. He would be one of twelve travelers. That seemed like the perfect group size. Best of all they would all be complete strangers.

As soon as he had a departure date, James returned THE BOX to Manjit and arranged for his personal items to be stored and the house rented out for two years.

CHAPTER ELEVEN

# SPRING 2010

The past two years had been a whirlwind for James. As each tour ended, he signed up for another one. He had seen the wonders of Asia, Africa, the Americas, Australia, and Europe.

Not only had he increased his knowledge of the history and geography of the world, he had learned some basic social survival skills. One important skill was how to be pleasant and companionable with strangers without divulging too much information about yourself. Because each tour had different participants, he was able to tell the story of his life without worrying about discrepancies. He didn't have much to worry about. It seemed the other travelers were also avoiding sharing personal information. Pleasantly aloof became his mantra. Avoid all alcohol and drugs so as not to lose control.

Now back at home, James felt ready to move on. It was time to hit the internet and newspaper archives to piece together what he could about finding his biological family, if any of them were still alive. James needed to discover if he wanted to carry on as James Matthew Oates or try being Robert (Bobby) Andrew.

His MaMa's diary had left enough clues for him to start. So far no one else knew the contents of THE BOX.

Before he left town, he had Manjit re-lease the house and file his income taxes for the last two years.

The best place to start his search seemed to be BC. James decided to take a page out of Julia's book, so he purchased a small RV that would allow him to travel west without worrying about hotel reservations or eating at diners all the time. Before he left town, he had a bike rack attached to his unit so he could explore trails along the way. He would park somewhere that had Wi-Fi and begin his research.

He thought he would start with Julia's family. It seemed less emotional. The names Teresa and Jake Cerny did not seem to lead anywhere. He typed in Rangeland and scoured through accidents. He found one small article about the accident that claimed the lives of Julia's husband and stepson. It wasn't much help. The only information was that the accident happened on the highway between Rangeland and Deer Lake. That was his next lead to follow.

With another search, he found lots of reports and letters to the editor about the accident in the archives of the local Deer Lake Newspaper. That news was soon surpassed by the death of Monika and Brad Andrew and the mystery of their missing child.

He checked the list of names he had for people involved in the case: Detective Frank Carson, lawyer Harold Nichols, a nurse named Mandy, and his grandparents, Flo and Doug Johnson.

Good places to start. Hopefully they were all still alive and in town.

Using the journal as a guide, James stopped at the places listed by Julia. He went to Virden, Qu'Appelle, and Gull Lake in Saskatchewan, then Strathmore, Alberta and Revelstoke, BC, staying one day in each place, trying to tease out any memory from over sixteen years ago.

Two weeks later, James drove close to the town of Deer Lake, stocked up on groceries, and set up his RV in the nearby Deer Lake Park. Physical activity was called for, so he hopped on his bike and rode for two hours, purposely avoiding the town site. Returning to the park, he cleaned up and made a meal.

While traveling with strangers for two years, James had learned that subtle probing during conversations can elicit a lot of information. He did not want to make direct inquiries in town, but knew he had to glean information about his past in a covert manner. Since it was off-season, there weren't many campers currently at the park. The manager was a talkative, friendly fellow who engaged James in conversation.

With a few simple questions, James learned that the owner, Chuck Olsen, had been born and raised in Deer Lake. He appeared to be around fifty and loved to brag about his town. James felt comfortable enough to do a bit of digging.

"Well, Chuck, you're obviously very proud of your town. It sure is a beautiful location. So tell me, what's the worst thing that ever happened here? A jaywalker, maybe a bank robbery?"

Chuck was so excited he nearly fell out of his chair. "I'll tell you young man, we have a big story here. Murder, suicide, possible kidnapping!"

"Wow," exclaimed James. "Details please!"

It took an hour, but Chuck told the story of Monika's suspicious death, Brad's suicide, and the missing child, Bobby. The car accident that killed Julia's family did not seem to be part of the story.

"Yeah," continued Chuck, "the town has never really let the story go. Detective Carson gets publicity on the story every year by publishing an age-enhanced photo of what Bobby might look like today."

At this point, James was happy he had grown a beard and started to wear sunglasses and a floppy hat. If, by chance, he resembled either of his birth parents, he didn't want to bring attention to himself.

Chuck was on a roll. He carried on, The Apex Auto Wreckers and Scrap Yard was sold and replaced with housing units. The Andrew family disappeared, and soon after, their daughter Kristie married and left town. The Johnsons went to a foreign country to do missionary work for the church."

James yawned deeply, told Chuck it was a fascinating story, and said he could continue it tomorrow. He bid the host good night and retired to his RV. He was afraid to appear too interested.

His first stop the next day would be to the local newspaper archives where he'd be able to find more information and details about the case. Then he had to find the tenacious Detective Carson, who apparently was still in town.

After a quick breakfast of cereal, James hopped on his bike, said hello to Chuck, and started off towards the town, looking for anything that might be familiar. He hadn't been here in over sixteen years, so some things would have changed.

He pedaled along Main Street past businesses he didn't recognize. Slowly, he weaved in and around the residential areas. At one point, he slammed on his brakes and got off his bike. He stared at a small house with a large yard full of children's toys. It was not totally familiar, but there was something about it that made him pause. Next to it was a fairly modern house that did not register with him at all. Not wanting to draw attention to himself, he got back on his bike and rode around some more. He stopped once again at a church, but it too was only vaguely familiar. It had obviously been renovated in the past few years.

Now he had to find the detective's house: 473 Aspen Court. He plugged the address into his phone.

It was time to face what had been haunting him all his life.

Gathering up all of his courage, James knocked on the door. It was opened by a tall grey-haired man.

"Yes, young man. How can I help you?"

James felt his chest tighten and tears come to his eyes. He was meeting the man who never quit looking for him. He had no idea how to react. The two men stood staring at each other.

Finally, in a raspy voice, James uttered, "I believe you have been looking for me. I am Bobby Andrew."

The detective didn't flinch. "You're not the first person to show up claiming to be Bobby. I will need some verification," said Frank, always the police officer.

James reached into his pocket and brought out a small card. He handed it to Frank. It was the birth certificate in the name of Robert Bradley Andrew.

"Oh my God! Where did you get this?" Frank demanded.

"It was in a safe belonging to my MaMa. When she died over two years ago, I was given a box with a lot of information about my past. This birth certificate was in the box," answered James.

"Please come in. I have something to show you."

Frank ushered James into the den where the walls were covered with various photos and articles of the only case he had not solved in his long career.

James stood transfixed as he stared at the pictures of himself from birth to age four, plus enhanced photos of him as he was thought to have aged. Pictures of Brad, Monika, his grandparents, and a missing child bulletin of himself lined the walls. Lists of clues, sightings, and other sources of information were pinned up with all sorts of notes added.

James realized that he was trembling. The picture that hit him the most was of the house he had stopped at earlier. Yes, now he remembered it as it had been.

"I know that place. It was blue and yellow. There was a tree house in the backyard and a garden and lawn with a basketball net. Dad taught me to play basketball."

The next photo showed an older home with a man on the sitting on the deck. The house had been replaced by a modern rancher. James stared at the picture of the house and the man sitting on the deck. He was fighting to find a long-lost memory. He knew he had spent time at that house but couldn't quite remember why.

His brain reeled with memories that he called out, astounding Frank with the accuracy. But Frank knew DNA tests would have to be done. Also, a clean shave and haircut would show Bobby's appearance more. Signs of Monika and the birth father might give clues.

As Frank was reverting to the role of investigator, James was trying to deal with his long-buried memories. His head and heart were throbbing. Tears formed in his eyes as he remembered a loving home and large extended family.

"I need to make a phone call to my friend Harry to share this news with him. He has stood by my obsession with this case all these years."

"Oh, would that be Harry Nichols, the lawyer?" asked James.

"What? How do you know that?" asked Frank in a stunned voice.

"My MaMa said he helped her a lot," answered a trembling James.

"And who would that be?" queried Frank, thinking immediately about his friend's quest for information about the vanishing Anne Novak from years ago. "What is your MaMa's name?" Frank asked while holding his breath.

"Julia Anna Novakova."

Frank knew that couldn't be a coincidence. The name was too similar to Harry's missing client, Anne Novak. Her case coincided with the Andrew case. He had to call Harry immediately. This young man may solve both their cases. Could Anne have taken Bobby? He quickly picked up his phone and called Harry. "Get over here now!" he literally screamed into the phone.

Within minutes, the door flew open and Harry appeared. He looked from Frank to James and back again.

Frank took a deep breath and said, "Meet Bobby Andrew."

Harry had to sit down. He stared at James. "What?" was all he could manage to say.

"He was abducted by your mystery woman, Anne Novak."

"What?" Harry repeated.

"Yes, both our mysteries could have been solved if we had connected the two disappearances," sighed Frank.

The three men shared their version of events with one another, repeating, reiterating, refining, and rethinking until they managed to piece together their stories. James told them of his MaMa's diary, which Frank and Harry both desperately wanted to read.

Since Coralee Carson and Leslie Nichols were away for the weekend, the men were left uninterrupted to continue their discussion. At one point, Frank went to the kitchen to throw together a few sandwiches. He grabbed a bottle of juice and three glasses before heading back to the den.

Meanwhile, Harry and James had been discussing Julia, the woman Harry knew as Anne. His vivid memory of the emotional trauma she had experienced brought great pain to James as he knew what a kind, loving woman she had been to him and to others

Over the years, other men had appeared on the scene claiming to be Bobby. Simple DNA and fingerprint tests proved them wrong. They all left in a hurry when threatened with charges of fraud. Frank explained to James that he too would have to take the DNA and fingerprint tests. Monika had Bobby fingerprinted at a seminar at daycare years before.

Frank did not want to raise any undue interest in the latest claim. He called Dr. Sean Tait, who had tested at least a dozen claimants over the years. Frank trusted his professional judgment and confidentiality. Despite feeling convinced that this young man was Bobby, Frank asked questions and made comments to try to find discrepancies. Bobby was only four when he left Deer Lake so it was safe to assume his memories would be vague, especially when Julia had sixteen years to dilute and remove his memories.

James filled the men in on his happy childhood full of love. On occasion, Harry or Frank would add a comment or ask a question. One way to illicit memories was to continue showing old photos and videos. Frank once again showed the interior and exterior photos of the home the Andrews had lived in. On seeing the exterior, James instantly recognized it, not only from distant memory but from hours ago when he had stopped in front of the house! It had changed somewhat over the years, but the basic house and yard had not. Then he remembered the other house. It was no longer there but his memory of it reaffirmed that he was, indeed, Bobby.

"That's Mr. Ralph's house. I brought him cookies and he gave me candies!"

Frank and Harry looked at each other. That was something only Bobby would know. Ralph Cornwallis had been an unreliable witness at the time of Bobby's disappearance. Had his memory of the events of the fatal day been more accurate, the story may have had a very different ending.

Next, James was shown pictures of the interior of the house. He did recognize the rooms and some items. That did not prove much as many of the pictures had been featured in print and on documentaries over the years. But it sure excited the two old friends. James could name the toys that were featured and identify other items. He recognized the wall and shelves that were filled with ribbons and trophies. That information had not been released at any time. He showed some signs of memory as family photos of birthdays and other holidays were displayed.

Soon they were all exhausted. James was sapped. Frank and Harry were also emotionally drained. They changed the subject and asked James about his life since he learned of his identity.

James talked about his two years of world travel in an effort to leave everything behind and focus on exploring the world at large.

Eventually, the room was silent. They were all over-whelmed by information so Frank and Harry decided it was time for a beer. James declined and headed out. It was late and he wanted to get back to the campsite. He jumped on his bike, stopped at a fast-food restau-rant, and inhaled a burger and fries before heading out in the dusk.

Once back at the campsite he went directly into his RV, purposely bypassing his host. He wondered what would happen next.

Finding answers to his repressed memories was making James feel unsettled. He always knew there was a mystery surrounding his childhood and had badly wanted to discover what it was. Now that he knew, it was a bittersweet feeling. Sweet, because he may now have a real family again. Not so sweet because he had lived in a fog for so long. He recalled how confused he felt when he read Julia's letter. He thought so much about her during his travels. His feelings went from empathy for her sad life to anger that she had kidnapped him. He was now feeling many things at once - happy, confused, and anxious. He really wanted to meet any of his relatives that were still around. He gave into a mix of happy exhausted tears.

He looked out and saw that Chuck was waiting for him at the campfire. He wanted to know James' impression of the town. Listening to Chuck carry on was the best medicine at this time. Sipping his cola and half listening to the older man talk gave James time to dwell on the few memories that had come to him during the day.

The next morning, before office hours, James was escorted into Dr. Tait's office for a quick checkup and DNA test. Not wanting to go back to the Carson's, he packed up the RV and drove to Rangeland. His first stop was to the cemetery where he located the three gravesites of Maria, José, and Matt Lopez. The area was immaculate. He felt a strange sensation knowing that he carried the name of the boy buried there. There lay the three people who first loved his MaMa.

When James left the graveyard, he decided to find the lawyer that had worked for MaMa. He scouted out the location and wondered what to do. What would he ask? What name would he use? He had birth certificates for two people his age. He had Julia's birth certificate as well. He decided the best thing to do was let Harry deal with Brent Summers, who appeared to still be running a law office.

Back in Deer Lake James biked around town and drove to various recreational spots where he watched teams play basketball, baseball, and soccer. He drove out to the lake to see the cottages on the beach that apparently played a big role in the Andrews and Johnsons lives. Many families were having fun in the lake and on the beach, but it did not stir any memories. On his bicycle, he explored every trail for kilometres around stopping to do exercises at the outdoor gym at Town Park. Vague rumors were floating around the town that another man claiming to be Bobby was in town. He tried to keep a low profile.

Two weeks later, he met with Frank, Harry and Dr Tait. DNA proved without a doubt that he was Monika's son. The fingerprints proved he was Robert Bradley Andrew. The scar on his leg was another identifier.

This was a huge story that would capture the attention not only of the town but all of Canada. Now that he knew the stories of Brad and Monika, James began to wonder if his biological father even knew he had fathered a child.

With his identity was now fully established, there would soon be a news conference to announce the end of an old mystery. But James still had many questions. Who would organize the news conference? How much information would be shared? Would Julia's relatives, the Cernys, surface? Or Erin Oates? Or the missing Andrew family? The Johnsons? His biological father? How would the people of Deer Lake, Rangeland, and Benson react? Would the fact of his wealth be revealed?

In the end, it was decided that since it was a police matter, the chief of police would make the initial announcement to select members of the local media.

The reporters arrived full of curiosity to find several notable locals seated at a large table. They noted Police Chief Daniels alongside retired Police Chief Frank Carson, Dr Tait, retired lawyer Harold Nichols, and an unknown bearded man in his early twenties.

Both reporters were very curious and couldn't wait to begin. Speculating with each other, they decided that with two retired people and a stranger there, it would have to be an old case. Could the mystery of the missing Bobby Andrew be solved?

The Chief stood and made the following announcement:

"After two decades, Robert (Bobby) Bradley Andrew has been found. DNA and fingerprints confirm his identity. He was abducted by Julia Anna Novakova, also known as Anne Novak. Anne was the surviving victim of a devastating car accident just before Monika

Andrew died. Bobby was raised in a loving home in Manitoba. Papers he found after the death of Julia led Bobby to the story of his disappearance. That is all I can offer at this time. You will be given a package of information on your way out." They grabbed the info packet and nearly tripped over each other as they ran from the room. Bobby was spirited away to a waiting car and driven to a private B&B away from town.

CHAPTER TWELVE

# SPRING 2010

The fallout was immediate. All media sources interrupted their current programs to share the breaking news. Instant experts were interviewed about the psychological impact of a kidnapped victim learning to love their captor. Experts on PTSD were offering an indepth understanding of Julia. People claiming to be best friends of all involved were interviewed. Other reporters kept repeating, "What we know at this time . . ." and of course, the overworked term "alleged."

James knew that he was now Robert Bradley Andrew and would begin using the name that had haunted him for years.

Bobby, still in disguise, was overwhelmed and avoided the media camp that had set up overnight. Harry agreed to be his agent, acting as the go-between with the press. He scheduled audio-feed interviews with the most trustworthy, professional reporters, including those from Benson. The initial frenzy paled after ten days, but life would never be the same.

Bobby and Harry contacted Manjit, who began the complicated process of having all James Matthew Oates' assets transferred to Robert Bradley Andrew.

Two weeks later, Harry Nichols, and Frank Carson were seated at a conference table when Bobby appeared, wondering what news they had for him.

The Cerny family had been located but had asked to be left alone. Their selfish role in Julia's life was now well known thanks to the work of investigative reporters. The Johnsons had contacted Frank with the understanding that he was not to reveal their where-abouts. Flo was not well. As much as she needed to see Bobby, she would wait for a while and hope the press would not find her.

Bobby decided to continue traveling as incognito as possible while things unraveled. His first step was to find a way to meet with the Johnsons, his only living family. Frank told him that they lived a quiet life in Montreal.

Knowing that photos of his appearance and his RV were on all forms of media, he left the RV with

Chuck, shaved his face and head, bought large glasses with tinted lenses, bought a cane, and started walking with a limp. He headed out with a backpack to travel by train to Quebec City, then by bus to Montreal. He needed to be cautious and not draw attention to himself.

***

As soon as Bobby was settled in a hostel in Montreal, he found the church that the Johnson's attended. He knocked on the rectory door and asked to see the priest. He was led to the office by the woman who had opened the door.

"Yes, young man, how can I help you?"

"My name is Bobby Andrew. Detective Carson told me to see you regarding the Johnsons."

"Oh yes, I've been expecting you. Please, come in and sit down. If you don't mind, show me your birth certificate. We just can't be too sure."

Bobby showed him the document.

"The Johnsons (known locally as Ellen and John) have heard that you have been found via news channels and talks with Frank but they don't know that you're in town. It was decided it would be best if we waited until we knew you were safely here. I'll call right now." The priest picked up the phone and dialed.

"Ellen, John, I have excellent news. Bobby is here with me. We will be at your place as soon as we can."

"Oh, praise the Lord. We will await your plans. A reporter has already been here, so we know a mob is coming."

"Okay, we will devise a plan to hide you. Get a few things packed and be ready to go."

The priest phoned three of his most trusted parishioners. They eagerly agreed to a ruse to spirit the Johnsons away from the press.

A patrol car drove to the house and asked all media to get off private property.

Four cars with covered license plates drove up to the Johnson house. Each driver jumped out wearing a Halloween costume and carrying a duffle bag then aided a costumed passenger out. Each passenger walked with two canes. All eight people hustled into the house. The door was closed briefly, then eight people in costume walked out. Four were using two canes. They got back into the cars and sped off. Once at the four way stop, the first three went in different directions. The fourth stayed behind the stop sign, stalled across the road, preventing the cars that were in hot pursuit from catching up to the others.

Once they knew they were not being followed, the priest, with Ellen as his passenger, drove to a home belonging to a church member. He assisted her into the house, got her settled in the den, removed his costume, then drove away.

Minutes later, a second car drove up and John hurried out, leaving two canes behind but carrying a duffle bag. The driver removed his mask and drove away. He quickly entered the den and rushed to Ellen, who was sobbing. They hugged each other. Once again, just like twenty years ago, their lives revolved around avoiding the press.

They had just begun to relax when they became aware of someone else in the room. John stared at a clean-shaven young man who also had tears in his eyes. It was their long-lost grandson. Cries of joy and anguish filled the room.

John rushed over to Bobby and held him at arm's length. The recognition was complete as he saw Monika's eyes staring back at him. The men embraced. They walked to Ellen who was sobbing and reaching her arms out to Bobby and calling his name.

They talked well into the night. Ellen and John, now again known as Doug and Flo told him of their never-ending belief that he was alive and well. They were relieved to know he was raised in a happy church-going home, not sold into child slavery. They spoke of the many missions they had managed.

Bobby was anxious to learn all that he could about the first years of his life. His grandparents poured out stories of love and happiness until the fatal day that

Brad discovered Monika had been unfaithful to him. The families could not accept that fact as Monika and Brad were so totally devoted to each other.

Bobby asked what his life would have been like if Julia had not taken him. According to her diary, when she picked Bobby up at the house, he was in a very drowsy state. Who would have raised him and where? Flo and Doug said that they would have assumed custodial rights over Bobby as they were his only blood relatives. They would leave town as Bobby would have always be surrounded by the stigma of being the child of a scandal. They also knew that wherever they went, they story would follow them. They had spent a lot of money on private investigators who followed every sighting and rumour. (Bobby thought that someday he would compare the sightings to the route Julia had taken to see if any of them were accurate.)

They returned to Canada to retire in the anonymity of a big city. Since they were both strongly bilingual, they settled on Montreal. The proceeds from the sale of their home, cabin, and business in Deer Lake had left them with a livable income.

To further cover their tracks, they assumed different first names. They figured Johnson was common enough and so they kept it. Flo's legal name was Florence Ellen Johnson, so she began her new life as Ellen Johnson. Doug, knowing that a lot of men with

Johnson as a last name were known as John, introduced himself as such.

At first, they rented a furnished apartment and immediately sought out a church. After a couple of months, feeling secure, they bought a small house and settled into retirement

Slowly, they became involved with a few committees at the church. They had a few close friends but always steered conversation away from their personal past. They needed to give a biography that was not a lie, but enough not to make anyone curious.

Frank was the only person from the past they kept in touch with as he was still pursuing every lead that came up when the aged enhanced photo of Bobby was released.

Then next morning, Bobby was up early and made a wonderful breakfast from the ingredients he found in the kitchen. The three continued to talk and exchange stories of the past years, but had to keep looking out the window to be sure no one had discovered them.

They turned on the TV to see a breaking news story about the discovery of the Johnsons. People they knew were being interviewed. Included were their stunned neighbours, the local merchants, and casual acquaintances who suddenly always suspected there was a story behind the Johnsons

Bobby's presence had not yet been discovered, although reporters were speculating that he was probably somewhere in the area. Sightings of him were reported constantly. The priest was tight lipped with his only answer being, "I have no comment." The couples that had helped with the escape were found and interviewed, also responding with "no comment."

Once again, instant experts were spouting rhetoric about kidnapped victims and Stockholm syndrome. Others suddenly remembered seeing Julia sixteen years ago as she rushed across the country. People from Rangeland suddenly claimed to have been her friend.

***

After touring the continent in their RV from Alaska to Baja, the Andrews decided to leave BC and Canada behind them. They purchased property in a gated community on the outskirts of Panama City and began life there as a retired couple, Jay and Marie Anders. Within a year, they were tired of the endless boring life there so sold out and moved into the city. To help fill their days, they both took jobs teaching ESL. They were soon part of a group of expats that did the same and did not question each other about the past. The unwritten rule seemed to be "ask not," as everyone had a story they would rather forget. Both of them still cried daily at the loss of the life they so enjoyed in Deer Lake. When the news of Bobby being found hit the TV in Panama, no one paid much attention and the news feed quickly disappeared. If any one of their acquaintances suspected anything, they never mentioned the possible connection.

Once they knew that Bobby had been certified as Monika's son, they wondered at all if he remembered them and the good life. Would they come forward and continue to stay out of his life? Would the Johnsons welcome them back as friends?

After weeks of agonizing, they decided to stay out of the story unless they found out through media that Bobby wanted to see them. Kristie and her husband Mark had settled in Alberta. They did not have any children. Every year, the two couples would meet somewhere in Central America to visit and share their love and heartbreak. Hopefully, no reporter would uncover their whereabouts. They continued their lives in self-declared exile, making the most of chances to find an hour or two of happiness now and then.

The Carsons and Nichols retired, sold their town-homes, bought RVs, and planned to spend the next few years as snowbirds, living six months at the cabin and six months on the road. The women were happy that their men had finally agreed to retire and head across Canada. What they did not know was that they had a copy of Julia's diary and copies of all the sightings that had been reported. They were on a quest.

***

Debra and Phil were sitting on the deck of their condo on the beach of an expensive gated community in Hawaii. They had retired from their careers as sex experts and were enjoying the good life.

"Well," said Deb, "here we are two of Deer Lake High's least favourite students. Mom would be so proud of me. I found something I enjoyed and did it better than anyone else. Not only that, but I still have my little book with names and pictures if we ever need it. Brad was one of the few businessmen in town that didn't visit me."

"Are you reminiscing because of the news from good old Deer Lake?"

They had just finished reading the Canadian news about the long-lost Bobby Andrew being found.

"So the lady that took Bobby was the one who survived the crash with my RV. Nice connection. She financed her escape with the money from my insurance! I wonder if they'll ever find the father. If not, Bobby will be just like me, never knowing who his father is," she added.

Phil turned to Debra with a smirk on his face and shocked her with his next comment.

"Well, I should do a DNA test to find out if I'm the father. Maybe he would share some of his enormous wealth with me."

Debra was so stunned that she choked on her drink. When she recovered, she let out a howling laugh.

"OMG! Phil, were you the mysterious person out behind the gym while Brad was being paraded? How come no one ever suspected you? I can't believe you got near the Virginal Princess of the school! This has made my life complete. It would even be better still if everyone knew. What shall we do? How in the world have you managed to keep that a secret?"

"It wasn't my finest moment. I have always been deeply ashamed of what I did. So far, Deb, we have made a good life for ourselves without hurting anyone. We have never used your special book and videos, so why would we hurt someone now?"

Reluctantly, Deb agreed. It would serve no purpose.

\*\*\*

Looking at the legal documents in front of him, Bobby's mind was racing. On the left was a birth certificate, passport, and driver's license saying he was James Matthew Oates. All of them were now null and void, and fraudulent, if used. On the right were a birth certificate and medical records stating that he was legally Robert Bradley Andrew. He had lived four halcyon years as Bobby Andrew and sixteen wonderful years as James Matthew Oates. Now he had decided who he wanted to be.

He would change his name to Julian Andrew Johnson. It recognized and honoured all the people who had loved him. It would also give him a new persona. Flo and Doug were overjoyed with his decision. It would take time and paperwork, but he wanted to start using the name sooner rather than later. He would also have a nickname-JJ.

Using some of his wealth, he purchased an estate in rural Quebec where he would live with the Johnsons until he mulled over the journey he had been on since Julia had died. First, he would travel for another year, being sure to stop in on his newly found Aunt Mavis and her family in Africa. His grandparents wished him well and sent their love with him. When he returned, he would begin a non-profit charity to assist Canadian families experiencing hardships.

\*\*\*

Along with his new name, Julian had a new look: a small mustache and a ponytail. He was the last passenger to deplane after a long flight from Canada to Germany to Monrovia, Liberia, Africa. He was so excited to be meeting the rest of his real family. He scanned the crowd of people greeting the returning passengers. Then his heart stopped briefly, and tears welled in his eyes as he spotted a woman carrying a sign saying **Hi! Bobby. Welcome.**

Julian had found Mavis, the next step on the road to discovery.

# AUTHOR'S NOTES

This novel began years ago in a dusty campsite on the outskirts of Yuma. It was put on the shelf while my husband Gerry and I traveled internationally to many countries. It was put on hold a second time when cancer intruded on our lives taking him and keeping me occupied for a few years. While packing up the house I found the manuscript. COVID gave me time to resurrect it. But it was harder work then I anticipated. Therefore, here I am two years later ready to send it to print even though I know it has a lot of potential to be an amazing novel.

Thanks to Diane Rutledge for her encouragement along the way.

Lenora Klappe

CPSIA information can be obtained
at www.ICGtesting.com
Printed in the USA
BVHW040802081122
650437BV00001B/1